Once Upon a Christmas

Stories by
James Dillet Freeman

Unity Books

Illustrations by E'Van Lattimer

Unity Village, Missouri 64065
Library of Congress Card No. 78-53345
Third Printing, 1984

Designed by Janna Russell

Contents

Preface

I hope you like long prefaces. If you don't, you can skip this one, for it will be long. I am going to talk about Christmas, my stories, and me.

How did I happen to write these Christmas stories? How did I happen to be me?

From my earliest memory I have been in love with Christmas and, as with everything one loves, a little fearful about it, fearful that it may disappoint me, fearful that somehow sometime it will not be there when I look.

No other day of the year has such power to stir and excite us—though Christmas is not just a day, it is a season. The year does not have four seasons, it has a fifth: Christmas. And Christmas is at least as long as the other four. I have seen springs that hardly lasted a week and falls that weren't much longer, while Christmas for most people begins no later than Thanksgiving Day when the lights go on in shopping centers, and lasts till Twelfth Night when we make a bonfire of the trees.

When you are a small boy, you are never unaware of Christmas, for you have been warned that Santa Claus or God or somebody is keeping a strict account of your misbehavior, and what you are going to get for Christmas depends on how bad you weren't. I was always threatened with coal—or perhaps it was switches—in my stocking. And since I knew I had been bad, I always got out of bed on Christmas morning with a great deal of anxiety. However, the stocking was always plumped with goodies.

Also, every year my parents debated whether or not they should have a tree. Probably the debate was meant to keep me on tenterhooks. If so, it succeeded. For I was never sure until I saw it in the parlor, resplendent with tinsel and baubles, that a tree would be there.

Also, though I kept up the pretense as long as I could, I think I knew from my earliest years that there really was no Santa, and so there really was the possibility that there wouldn't be a Christmas. That's a frightening thought for most of us children, isn't it?

What with all my fevers of expectation, deliriums of imagination, and fits of fear, I was usually sick by Christmas, with an upset stomach and a runny nose. I am glad to say that the holiday no longer affects me so disastrously.

If some of you who read my writing have thought that I have always been a perfect model of spiritual composure, alas, you know now that it has taken me years of prayer just to calm down Christmas. Maybe that's because at heart I am still a very small boy (if you ask my wife she will tell you there is no doubt about that); one would have to be to write poetry—or Christmas fables!—in a world that seems to have sold its soul to its advertising men and expects to be saved by science.

These ten stories are only a small part of what I have written about Christmas. I have written at least twice that many articles and at least fifty or sixty poems, some short, some not so short.

Remember, I have worked at Unity School of Christianity almost all my adult life. And Unity School publishes magazines, and those magazines always have a December issue. I don't believe anybody in the publishing business has ever put out a December magazine without Christmas in it.

So editors here have always been delighted that they had this Christmas-crazed boy handy. All they had to do was wave a picture of a candle or a fir tree or almost anything Christmasy in front of him and whisper, "It's Christmas, Jim, can you write something?" and very shortly out would come at least a short piece of Christmas verse.

One of the first pieces of writing I ever did for Unity was a Christmas verse I wrote for Silent Unity to send to correspondents. It was called "Your Christmas Guest." I did not sign my name to it, just Silent Unity. It was reprinted so many times by different organizations that finally people wanted to know who wrote it.

For more than forty years I do not believe there has been a Christmas when I have not written at least one piece, prose or verse—and usually several pieces—about Christmas. Do not get the idea I have written just on demand. I have written because I love Christmas—and Unity! I have written dozens of Christmas things that have never been published; I wrote them because I wanted to write them; some thought or incident sparked my inspiration and I wrote.

However, it is only recently that I have written stories. For one thing, Unity periodicals did not seem to me to invite stories, and also, I liked writing poetry—or prose that was like poetry.

Telling you how I write and how I happened to start writing these stories—as well as I can remember—may give you a little insight into the curious and unforeseeable way in which the creative process works.

I remember clearly how I wrote the first fable. I had been asked to read some of my Christmas poetry to a business women's group in Lee's Summit. The meeting was on a Sunday afternoon in a church. After I read my poems, I was anxious to get away as soon as I could, because the Chiefs—Kansas City's football team—were playing an out-of-town game and I wanted to watch them on television. I can't remember whether they won or lost the game, for as I watched it, my thought kept drifting back to Christmas. I fell to thinking about the birth of Jesus and how it took place—in a stable, of all places! I have always loved that. I got to thinking about the animals in the stable. There is a legend that when Jesus was born, the animals that were present at His birth were given the power of speech so that they could praise Him; and ever since on Christmas Eve at midnight the animals in the barnyard can speak. As I thought about the legend this poem began to form itself in my mind:

At Christmas a spell is said to steal
At midnight over all dumb things
So that any of them that would can kneel
For a moment under angel wings.

And an angel song will fill their throats
Till they sing as none before have sung.
Lord, when You teach dumb things their notes,
Will You not touch my stumbling tongue?

For I, Your human creature, come
On a night when there is no star to see,
And kneel and wait like all things dumb
For the angel song to be sung in me.

After I had written the poem, I continued to think about the animals. I wondered which ones had been there, and I began to count them off: donkey, ox, sheep, goat, these certainly—perhaps some chickens and geese, and surely a mouse or two, and a few birds flying in the loft. Suddenly I thought: Whatever animals might have been there, there is one that could not have been present—the pig! Jesus' family was Jewish.

Immediately my heart went out to the little pig that could not have been there, and in a matter of minutes I was writing "The Tale of a Pig."

Oh, I don't mean it was written in minutes. As I recall, it took weeks. I lavished every skill I had on it. Writing it was a labor of love.

But once I had it written, I did not know what to do with it. I have never been much at marketing. I have no agent, and they are indispensable if you are going to sell what you write. Agents don't care for poets; they bolt the door and lock the windows when they hear that one is in the neighborhood.

Once I talked to my editor at Doubleday about printing my poetry; he shuddered, bared his teeth, and hissed: "You can't sell the stuff. We print fifteen hundred volumes, and palm off a thousand of them on bookstores. With luck they sell maybe five hundred, and send the other five hundred back to us." I also talked to him once about my Christmas stories. He shuddered in the same way, made the sign of the cross, and backed out of the room.

But I had enjoyed writing the first story—oh, I truly had! If you have never written something that is pure imagination, you can't know the sheer delight of concentrating as intensely as you can on something that is and isn't at the same time, letting your mind soar to catch ideas you did not even know were there until you caught them, excitedly pouring out and dubiously stumbling over words, and slowly seeing something formless find a form, something that was not there until you put it down, something so elusively illusion that sometimes you, the author, do not know what it is going to be until you have written and rewritten it and have the final words on paper and have read it.

I enjoyed writing the first story so much that I wrote a second one, this time about an "Angel with a Broken Wing."

I am not sure from what obscure source the idea for it first filtered through. Perhaps it was from a joke about an angel with a broken wing one of my students had told me years before the thought occurred to me to write a story about such an angel. The joke had nothing to do with the story, but I had never forgotten it. I make speeches on religious subjects, and there seem to be very few religious jokes. At least I have heard only a few. So any I hear are never forgotten, not if there is even a remote hope they can be repeated in church; most of them can't.

Jokes are an absolute necessity for any speaker who hopes to keep his audience awake without having the ushers walk up and down the aisles with a padded pole and thump anyone they see nodding (a device New England preachers used 200 years ago). When I decided to become a speaker, my first act was to buy a joke book.

Laughter, I have felt, should be held almost as holy as prayers. God, I am certain, has a sense of humor. He would have to have. To make people smile—surely this must be one of the most sacred acts a human being can perform.

But as I said, the joke had nothing to do with the story except that it planted an angel with a broken wing in my mind. My mind was already full of angels.

I have always loved the thought of angels. Unbelievable as it may seem to you—most of the time it seems unbelievable to me—I believe in them.

Most of my Unity friends say that angels are winged thoughts. Zarathustra, who almost invented angels, named his chief archangel Vohu Manah, Good Thought. And I won't argue that this is what angels are. But who shall say what forms thoughts may assume? Anything from gods to galaxies, no? But the question then becomes, are the gods and galaxies thoughts or are the thoughts gods and galaxies?

I won't say what angels look like, but oh, I can tell you how they feel. They feel reassuring.

I know this makes me hopelessly out of touch with the times, but I would rather be medieval and look for angels, winged and singing, than be modern and look for little green men in a flying saucer from Mars.

I even think I have known a few angels. They looked just like us and they never told me they were angels; perhaps they did not know. It may be that when an angel takes human form, one of the conditions is that the angel will not remember what he or she was before, just as we don't remember if we have lived before.

It would not surprise me at all to find I have a guardian angel. God knows I have needed one! At a number of critical times in my life, I have been protected against myself and my own stupid desires, and have made decisions wiser than I intended to make. I often feel angels very close. Sometimes this has been embarrassing. I hope they are polite enough to know that on occasion they need to depart on some heavenly errand or at least turn away, shut their eyes, and pray. But then I am sure they expect me to be human as I expect them to be angelic.

I am always looking for them—or not so much looking as listening. I think when God has something to say He sends an angel. Many times I wake at two or three o'clock in the morning, and lying there in bed, I say, "God, have You anything to say? If You do, I'll be glad to get up and put it down." Then I lie there and listen. And it has been amazing how often when I listen, I hear. It's hard on sleep but wonderful for the inspiration. As a matter of fact, I got up at three o'clock this morning and it's four as I write this.

Since I've always had this warm feeling about angels, it was natural that I should write about them, especially when I wanted to write about Christmas. Angels and Christmas have much in common—or should I say, uncommon? They go together like April and rain, May and flowers, June and weddings.

Naming the angel did not occur until I was writing the story, and of course the moment he told me his name the story took a different course.

The boy in the story, Johnnie, and his brothers were real children. I was at their home one wintry day, and the football game in the snow, with Johnnie in his bare feet and his brothers pummeling him, actually took place. Perhaps as I heard the father exasperatedly tell me that Johnnie just wasn't like his brothers, the story began to take form.

You can see from this what unrelated incidents—a joke about an angel, some brothers playing football in the snow—somehow are brought together in the mind to make a story. I guess it's a lot like the way a cook creates a dish. The cook may throw into the pot anything from a rabbit to a radish and a touch of nutmeg, but when these are stirred together, out comes, not separate ingredients, but a single succulent delight.

I wrote these first two stories, "The Tale of a Pig" and "Angel with a Broken Wing," just for the joy of writing them. I had no idea where or whether they might be published. It did not occur to me that Unity would consider printing them; they never published fiction, and certainly no fiction like mine. My Doubleday editor told me once: "Our salesmen have a hard time selling your books. They can't tell the bookseller what shelf to put them on—whether they're religion or fairy tales, prose or poetry, for children or adults." I understand how he felt; I'm not sure myself.

But it happened that the editor of UNITY Magazine was fond of my writing. I often shared some of my writing with him that I knew he would not print in UNITY. One day I happened to tell him about these Christmas stories. He said he would like to read them, so I let him have them. Much to my surprise, he told me, "Jim, I'm going to keep 'The Tale of a Pig' and print it next Christmas in UNITY."

But the editor was required to temporarily leave the magazine. His assistants did not want to print the story—UNITY Magazine had never carried anything like this! Still, they felt they had to. So they buried it back in the magazine and cut it up on every page with blue-lined boxes containing profound quotations from Emerson and Kierkegaard—that way the page was not entirely wasted; it had a foolish fable on it, but also it had some serious thoughts.

However, a lot of readers liked the story; more wrote to the editor about the story than about anything else in the magazine. This surprised his assistants. It did not surprise me, even though, as I say, I too had wondered if the story belonged in UNITY. I expect people to like what I write. I get a kick out of writing it, so I think you'll get a kick out of reading it. I am capable of smiling or weeping when I read what I have written, just as I hope you are.

It surprises me when people write and say they don't like what I have written; I am sorry to say, this occasionally happens; some have even canceled their subscriptions.

Writing is an emotional task for me. I write—and rewrite—with a lead pencil. Words and phrases come gushing or dribbling out, some sparkling, some dull, some instantly recognized as right, some struck through almost as they are written down. My writing may be so marked through and written over that sometimes when I finally start to type it, I can hardly decipher the words or string the sentences together in a sensible order.

I do not outline, so I am not sure where I am going until I get there. Some of you with especially logical minds may be declaring, "Oh, how I wish he would!" But as I have said, I depend on my angels to be my guides—remember, they have wings!—and so at times I may find myself touching some thought far above my reach.

I don't mean that I abandon logic. Clarity is a passion with me. Few writers this side of comic books use shorter words or simpler sentences, though there is a hundred-word sentence in this Preface that may make you question this. I try to write so that you can interpret what I have written without having to run to a dictionary or a grammar book. I want to make my meaning clear.

But meaning is not enough. I want my meaning to sound like a music, and not only to speak clearly to your mind but to sing exultingly in your heart.

Anyway, when a lot of people told UNITY's editor they liked "The Tale of a Pig," he told me he was going to print "Angel with a Broken Wing," too. I asked him if he wanted me to send him the manuscript, but he said that I wouldn't have to. He had made a copy when he had it, as he was sure the stories would be popular.

So the next Christmas he printed "Angel with a Broken Wing." Then he said to me, "Now your Chirstmas story is a Unity tradition. Our readers will look for them. I expect you to give me a Christmas story each year."

And so I have—ten of them.

People often ask me which of my stories I like best. I suppose I have my favorites, but even if I were sure, I wouldn't tell.

The one I got the most fun out of having written—it is not my favorite—is "An Event of Major Importance." The story upset some readers. Some liberal thinkers wrote that I had set back religion with such a literal, fundamentalist version of the story, and some fundamentalists wrote that I was desecrating Christian tradition. I liked all these letters because they showed I was reaching people of various religious viewpoints.

But an advertising man wrote me the letter I thought fit the story best. He said he was reading along, enjoying the story, and then he came to the last sentence. He wrote, "I did a quick double-take. Then I let out a roar and I cried out, 'Writing can be fun!' " I feel it ought to be.

If you read this story, don't, don't read the ending first. I have a horrible habit myself of picking up a book or magazine and reading from the back forward; a scanner and searcher for ideas, I go along hopping and scratching and occasionally alighting. I hope you don't have this affliction; it may be an alright way to read articles, and maybe even poems, but it wrecks stories.

But aside from the fun of writing such a story, the story had an unanticipated effect on some of its readers. Scores wrote me saying they were sure I had not just written a fable, that I was describing an actual event and they would like more information about it. Several told me they had seen the heavenly phenomena I had witnessed. I began to wonder. Do you suppose I was describing something that really had taken place?

Three of the stories deal with the birth of Jesus.

"The Tale of a Pig" is an animal fable, a pure wonder tale.

"A Conversation at an Inn" is a philosophical dissertation of sorts on the nature of Jesus, Christ, and God. It is my three Wise Men, except I make them three friends—the innkeeper, a Roman centurion, and a Persian merchant. Thus, I can discuss the event from the standpoint of the ordinary man of affairs, the logical thinker, and the mystic.

The third story, "My Name Is Joseph," is a love story. I have always had a special feeling for Joseph—a man's feeling for a man, I suppose. The Bible shunts him into a corner, as if he weren't important. And of course he is. He was asked to have a great deal of love and abundant understanding, and to accept what no man would find easy to accept.

There are a number of stories about Joseph in the apocryphal literature. Before I wrote my story, I read these, but accepted or rejected the material in them as I felt led. Most of these made him very, very aged, so old there could be no doubt that he was merely an appendage, Mary's husband only in name. But I made him the robust carpenter there is every reason to believe he was; Jesus, according to the Bible, had brothers and sisters.

I don't remember now where I got the idea for the story about Rosa.

The idea for "Are You Sure It's Snowing Beyond the Next Corner?" came to me out of a visit to Philadelphia. I had gone there to speak, but the deadline on my Christmas story was not far away, so undoubtedly my mind had its antenna up as far as I could raise it, searching for something to write about. And I believe my wife had said to me, "Why don't you write a love story?"

My mind is constantly sweeping the visible and invisible ethers; I am never without a pad and pencil—I won't buy a shirt that has no pockets—and now I also carry a small recorder. I put down any lines and phrases that happen my way on slips of paper that I squirrel away in manila folders. Especially when I have an assignment and the hour to deliver draws near and nothing has yet come, my mind races back and forth in a fluster of anxiety and expectation, probing into every unlikely corner, turning over any unlikely stones—sermons have been found in them, it has been observed—and above all looking hopefully to God—or at least, my angels. I have had ideas come singing into my head from the most unlikely sources and at impossible times. It is a very happy experience to have something start to write itself in your head at four o'clock in the morning when at eight o'clock you have to deliver a finished piece of writing.

In Philadelphia I went to eat one evening in a very old restaurant not far from the Delaware river. The restaurant had a romantic atmosphere. It was easy to imagine that I was in colonial times—and that is what I did.

I wrote "The King of Heaven Is Coming Tonight" because I wanted to tell a story about a scarecrow. The scarecrow appealed to me just as the little pig had. I felt how lonely and rejected he would feel out there in the middle of a winter field. When one writes, sometimes one gets carried away with what he is writing. I am moved by the characters in my stories; I can cry and laugh at what they experience—maybe if I didn't, nobody else would.

Once the thought of writing about a scarecrow came to me, I carried him tenderly around in my mind for a couple of years before I actually tried to embody him in words. When at last I sat down to my desk, the only part of the story that gave me any trouble was the opening section with the animals; once the little mother appeared on the scene with her baby, the story almost wrote itself. That is the way I like to write, but I am willing to write, no matter how long or how much rewriting it takes to get the writing done the way I want it—though I suppose it is never wholly the way I want it.

As with the scarecrow, I wanted to write "The Woman Who Learned to Love Christmas" for a couple of years before I wrote it. As I have said, I love Christmas. Many people rail at it as too commercial. And it is commercial. Christmas is as worldly as it is holy; it mixes the secular and the religious so that we cannot tell them apart. But isn't that the way we would like things to be? Wouldn't it be a better world if things were like that all year long? If every day had something of religion in it, and religion had something of every day? If we took the gaily wrapped gifts, the cards, the decorations in the stores and streets, Christmas trees, and Santa out of Christmas, as some people would like to do, it would no longer be Christmas. It might be wholly holy, but it would also be very dull.

There are even those who would take the wonder out of the wonder-tale itself, if they could. They dissect the language of the Bible to show that the writers did not really mean to say that Mary was a virgin; she was merely a maiden. And every year a scientist or two proves that the Star was not an unexplainable glow in the sky, but a conjunction of planets, or a nova recorded by Chinese astronomers, or something equally dull and reasonable.

I say leave Christmas alone. Christmas is a wonder and a magic, meant to cheer the heart, not argue with the mind. And that is what it ought to be.

So you "eat too much, drink too much, spend too much—and afterward wish you hadn't," as Ms. Darlington declares. Perhaps on occasion the human spirit needs to burst beyond its decorous and sensible bounds, and what better moment can it pick than this, when winter days are at their shortest and grayest and the nights are chilly and long. (My apologies to Australia, but perhaps there is no less need of such a gala moment when the humid heat of summer seeps across our souls. For hundreds of years Midsummer's Eve was a celebration almost as festive as Christmas, and why do you think we enjoy Fourth of July fireworks and picnics in the park?)

Christmas sends Santa—the glorious grandfather of us all—out across the empty skies to bring gifts to every child in the world. There has to be something more than self-concern in the human heart to make us dream up such a warm and selfless old fellow! There he stands before us—on street corners, in shopping centers, in stores—and we have at least to stop and consider, no matter how miserly we may be, the holy duty and the human joy of giving!

Christmas is a time of feasting, and if we can, we feast; but also Christmas makes us aware that there are hungry and shelterless and lonely people in the world. It prompts us to reach at least into our pockets, if not into our hearts, to share our feast with them.

Christmas brings the green tree into our house—yes, even if today it is pink and artificial—and loads it with ornaments. To come downstairs when you are three and see in the corner, which the night before had been bare, a Christmas tree laden with baubles and glowing with lights—will life ever offer a more magic moment?

Christmas makes us add a touch of color to our everyday rooms and everyday life, and puts a bright wreath or at least a green sprig on our front door as if we would say to all the world that there live in this house warm people who delight in beauty and believe in joy, and want to share a little of it with you—you would be welcome if you should come in.

Christmas makes us turn from our electric incandescence back to candles. Candles cast a very small light, but it is a light by which we may see one another's inner worth and beauty. Though it cannot warm our hands, it warms our hearts.

And even the jostling hurly-burly of the shopping centers—oh, I am sure we can thank our commercial instincts for them, but who is so dull of soul that he would not like to make at least one Christmas trip to one of them. For we go not only to buy, but also to satisfy our deep desire to rub elbows and spirits with our fellows, to press close and be pressed close into the bosom of humankind.

The festival of wonder, Christmas above all celebrates imagination.

That is what the story of the boy in "Imagination, Imagination!" is about, isn't it?

The boy in the story, I suppose, is myself. The story has elements of fact in it—part confession, part parable—but like all the other stories in this book it is a work of imagination.

For this is the kingdom and the power and the glory of imagination. It does not depend on the things we have, costly and beautiful and various though these may be; the things we have depend on it.

Perhaps some such Christmas as is described in the story is at least one of the reasons I write about Christmas.

And that is what I hope Christmas will always be, the celebration of imagination, with its power to warm our heart on a snowy day and sprinkle glitter on a dark one, to give us the goodwill to wish a merry Christmas though there is not much to feel merry about, to give us the faith to believe that life is not humdrum existence, but is capable of unbelievable wonder, and in the stable that is the human heart God Himself may make His appearance.

James Dillet Freeman

The Tale of a Pig

WHEN THE BABY was born in the stable, what a commotion broke out in the yard! All the animals who lived there were in a flutter and fuss. It was not every night that a baby was born in their stable, and certainly not such a baby as this.

The little pig who belonged to the innkeeper's neighbor was just as excited as any of the animals that belonged to the innkeeper. He lived in the field on the other side of the fence, but he spent so much time in the stable yard that he almost had to be counted as one who lived there. The fence was very old and he was very young, and to the young, a fence is not so much a barrier as a challenge.

Tonight the fence hardly seemed to be there. The little pig kept wriggling through it and under it and around it and asking the other animals: "What's happening now? What's happening now?" He could see for himself what was happening, but he asked—not because he wanted to find out but because he wanted to talk about it.

That this was a very wonderful happening there could be no doubt. Not only the animals knew it; the innkeeper and his wife kept bustling back and forth all night long, and when they were not coming or going they were sending the servants, one of them shouting at another, and all of them shouting at the stableboy posted at the stable door, who became so flustered that he baaed at the hens, and clucked at the sheep, and shooed the animals in and then shooed them out again.

For one thing, there was a star. It had come sailing out of the east till it reached the stable. There it stopped and stood, and shone right down on the roof.

"I tell you," said the turtle, whom all the animals respected as the oldest creature in the neighborhood, "not even when Julius Caesar was born—and there were some capital goings-on in the sky that night—was there anything like this."

The star was so bright that the cock flew up to the top of the stable and would have started to crow, thinking it was dawn, had not the owl who lived in the hayloft flown by and hooted at him that he was making a fool of himself.

The goat, who thought of himself as a scholar because he devoured every book he came upon, had an explanation. Tugging at his beard, he told the pig: "An extraordinary phenomenon, to be sure. But perfectly natural to us scientists. A conjunction of planets, we call it."

But there was not only the star, there were also the angels. Not even the goat was learned enough to explain away the angels; and it was what they were saying that stirred up most of the excitement. For they were saying that the baby who had just been born in the stable and was lying in a manger, wrapped in swaddling cloths, was Savior and Lord and was to be king of Israel. The angels flew in and out of the stable and they sang as they flew.

The little pig felt afraid when he first saw the angels; but after a while, as their huge wings billowed over him, softly rising and falling, he found himself feeling much as he remembered having felt before he was weaned, when he had nestled under the great warm body of his mother.

Later, when he and the other animals were talking about the night and trying to recall the angel voices, they asked the barnyard fowl—since they were singers of a sort—what the singing had been like; but, try as they would, the barnyard fowl could not describe it. Finally, a little barn swallow said that once on a journey he had alighted, weary from his long day's flight, by the edge of a wood where wild plum trees were blooming at twilight, and there while he rested a thrush began to sing. "It was like a hush within a hush," he said. "The angel song was like that, only more so."

One of the strange things about the star and the angels' song was that travelers staying at the inn slept soundly in their warm beds and rose the next morning and continued on their journey, unaware that anything at all had happened. But shepherds keeping sheep in distant fields saw the star and heard the singing and made the long trip through the dark hills to the stable.

As the little pig later told the cat, there are those who have eyes and see, and there is the rest of the world. There was no doubt in which group he belonged.

Or for that matter, any of the animals.

Human beings, being reasoning creatures, sometimes pass by wonders because their minds refuse to accept what they have come to believe runs contrary to their reason. Animals, on the other hand, hardly ever think about whether things seem reasonable or not. To them everything is a wonder. So they are attuned to wonders.

The moment the animals found out that the baby had been born, they all wanted to have a look at him. But they could see—what with so many angels and inn people and shepherds coming down from the hills—it would never do for all of them to crowd in at once. This was not just a baby, this was a king!

So they decided to go in one at a time. All agreed that the ox should be first, for it was in his manger that the little king was lying.

When he came out, all the animals were waiting.

"What is he like?" they cried.

"I have never seen any brand new babies before, and certainly none who is to be a king, but he is a boy baby," said the ox slowly. "I imagine he looks much like he ought to. He looks—uh—strong and well. Strong and well. There is only one thing."

"What is that?" asked the others.

"I thought he looked sad," said the ox.

"It is perfectly natural for a baby to look that way right after it is born," said the cow, who had been a mother many times and was considered to be an authority on the subject. "It will soon pass."

The animals were relieved to hear the cow say this; and in they came, one after another, to see for themselves what the baby king looked like.

The cows came. The sheep came. The goats came. The donkey came. In came all the barnyard fowl, the chickens, the ducks, the geese, and the guinea fowl. And of course the dog and the cat came; they came and went as they wished.

The turtle who lived in the pond came. The mouse who had a hole in the hayloft crept out onto a beam and peered down. And the birds who lived in the ceiling rafters—six pigeons, two swallows, three bats (they thought of themselves as birds), eight sparrows, and an owl—flew down to catch a view; but there was such a crowd of angels that the birds had to dodge between the big wings.

A few things came stealing out of the wild. A deer, a wolf, a rabbit, and a fox crept silent and unseen into the stable yard. They were too shy to go into the stable; but when the stable door flew open, the wolf leaped up and cried: "I saw him! I saw him!"

The other three all declared that they had seen him, too, and each tried to say what he looked like.

"He has lovely long ears!" said the rabbit.

"He has sharp white teeth!" said the wolf.

"He has soft brown eyes!" said the deer.

"What I like about him," said the fox, "is that he looks so much like me. It wouldn't surprise me at all if when he grows up he has red hair. Red hair is a mark of intelligence, you know."

The wolf mumbled under his breath that red hair—in the fox's case, at least—was the mark of an egotist. But he said nothing aloud; for some unaccountable reason he found himself feeling uncommonly friendly just then, even toward the fox.

"There is an old legend," said the fox, "that when this baby comes at last into his kingdom, the lion will lie down with the lamb."

"An old wives' tale is what it sounds like to me. I don't see much likelihood of that coming to pass, do you?" said the wolf, smiling at the deer and rubbing his shoulder against him affectionately.

And this is one of the strangest events of that strange night—as the deer and the wolf and the fox and the rabbit walked away, they walked side by side.

All the animals, as they came in, came in quietly; most of them tiptoed. They smiled at the mother, who was very young, and she smiled shyly back at them. They smiled at the baby, who was younger still, but he did not smile.

It was as the ox had said. The baby looked sad.

It troubled the animals to see the baby who was to be a king looking so sad, but in they came to bless him and be blessed; in they all came.

All, that is, except one. There was one who did not get in.

This was the little pig.

It was natural enough, I suppose, when you think about it, looking back.

After all, the land where all this was happening was Judea, and everyone knows that the baby's people—well, they just have never felt close to pigs.

But the little pig did not know this.

When he heard that the baby who was to be a king had been born, he was so happy he danced. His heart danced; his eyes danced; his ears danced; his tail danced; he danced deep down inside himself; and he kicked up his heels and danced a happy jig.

He rushed to get in line. He stood, impatiently but politely, until it was his turn to go inside. At last he reached the stable door.

But inside the door stood the stableboy. Beside the stableboy stood the innkeeper. Beside the innkeeper stood the innkeeper's wife. When the innkeeper's wife saw the pig, she shrieked. When the innkeeper heard his wife shriek, he called. When the stableboy heard his master call, he picked up a long stick and ran toward the pig.

"Hoo there! Hoo, hoo!" shouted the boy. "Get out of here, you pig!" And he gave him such a whack with the long stick that the little pig squealed with fright and scampered back across the stable yard and into the field where he lived.

There he lay, peeping through the fence and watching people and angels and animals coming to the stable.

Once he tried to slip back. This time when the stableboy saw him, he set the dog on him. The dog ran after him, barking ferociously. The little pig ran as fast as he could, for he was terrified, but the dog ran even faster; as he squirmed through the fence, he felt the dog's sharp teeth scrape his heels.

"See that you stay there," said the dog sternly. "You ought to know pigs aren't welcome here. From now on this stable is off limits for the likes of you."

When the dog saw how sad the little pig looked, he felt sorry for him. He did not particularly like pigs, but he prided himself on not having prejudices. So he said: "Don't feel too bad. They won't let the skunk in either."

This did not make the pig feel better, however. He did not think it was necessary for the dog to mention him in the same breath with the skunk.

When the dog had gone, the little pig lay there.

He had never felt so alone in all his life. He would have cried if he had known how, but his eyes had never learned to form tears. So he cried inside, where no one else could hear and no one else could know how much he hurt.

It was not that he was altogether surprised. His mother had tried to get him to stay out of the stable yard. "You're not wanted over there," she had told him. "You live in a part of the world where a lot of people have a prejudice against us pigs."

"Why?" asked the little pig.

"No reason," his mother had said. "You don't need a reason when you have a prejudice."

But the little pig had not really listened. His ears had heard her, but not his heart. No matter how much someone else has tried to make it plain, you never understand what something like this means until it actually happens to you.

Oh, several times he had caught hints and whispers!

Once the cat had told him, "You know, you're not a bad fellow for a pig," and another time as he came bouncing up, he thought he had heard the goat say to one of the ducks, "Some of my best friends have been pigs, but they do have a certain smell, don't they?"

But he had preferred to believe that he had not heard correctly.

The little pig had always looked pretty good to himself. At one end he had a long, pointed pink nose that he could wiggle, and at the other end he had a pink corkscrew tail that he could wiggle, too. In between he had sharp blue eyes that twinkled and danced, and sharp pink ears that sometimes stood up and sometimes flopped over, and a pink little roly-poly barrel of a body that squirted over the ground on four short, sturdy legs. Compared to a duck or a camel—especially a camel!—he thought he looked handsome.

He came from a fine old family. He had thrilled when his mother told him the story of his great-uncles; he liked her to tell it over and over. They were very famous, those three little pigs who had built their houses of straw and wood and brick, and outbraved, outwitted, and outlasted the big bad wolf in their world-renowned contest of bravery and brainpower. "They have been heroes as long as children have had heroes," his mother had told him.

His mother had told him, too, about another famous great-uncle—the fierce wild boar who at the end of a mighty hunt had turned and killed Adonis, the handsome young huntsman who was the lover of the goddess Venus. This act had made the goddess so angry that she had almost brought an end to life on earth. Tonight, as the little pig lay alone in the field and nursed his anguish, he wished he were like this uncle.

"All of us pigs should grow up to be like him," he thought. "Then they'd wish they had treated us differently," and he felt inside his mouth with his tongue to see if perhaps his tusks had begun to grow.

What a night! One moment he felt angry. The next moment he felt afraid. The next moment he felt crushed. The next moment he felt abandoned. The next moment he felt worthless. Every moment he felt miserable. It was the longest and saddest night of his short and merry life. "This night will never end," he said.

But at last the sun came up, the star faded, and the angels flew away. The cock flew up to the top of the roof and crowed, and the usual day that follows every other day began.

What a gabbling, honking, quacking, cooing, squawking, squeaking, chirping, lowing, braying, baaing, mewing, barking filled the stable yard! The king of Israel was asleep in the stable! (Though it is a wonder he got any sleep.) But whenever anyone peeped into the stable to see how things were, he came back to report that the baby was sleeping soundly, as a baby ought to do.

But also—of this there was no longer any question—the baby looked sad.

All that day the animals kept watch, each one hoping to be the first to catch the baby smiling. But he did not smile.

He looked at everything with eyes which were very kind; the cow who had very kind eyes herself said that the baby's eyes were kind.

But they were as sad as they were kind.

The animals had different ideas as to why he looked so sad.

"As you all know," said the ox, "I groan and sweat under heavy burdens that are piled on my back, until sometimes I think my back will break. When I looked at the baby, I thought I heard him say, 'Cast your burden on me, all you who are heavy laden,' and I—oh, I felt ashamed, but I could not help myself—I cast my burden on that little baby, and somehow I knew that all the burden-bearers of this world were casting their burden on him. Then I knew why he looked sad."

The old gander who lived in the pond told them: "Once when I was a young wanderer, I was hurt and left behind when the other geese flew south. The autumn rains fell chill across the dismal northland marshes. After the rain came the snow. When I looked into the baby's eyes, I remembered what it was like flying at night through falling snow, when there was no moon or star in the empty winter sky and I had to find my way alone. Then I knew why he looked sad."

The dog had his own thought. "Most of you don't know what it is to love," he said. "We dogs are known for the depth of our affection. We don't love many, but we love one or two. And we love them fiercely, devotedly; we lay down our life for them, willingly. When the baby looked at me, I felt how he loves everything more than I love anything. I could not myself feel such love, but I could sense what it must be like. Oh, what it must be like to have to love everything! Then I knew why he looked sad."

"All of you are right," said the donkey. "But when the baby looked at me, I felt he was not only looking at me, but through me and beyond me. And he saw something I could not see. He saw the suffering of things and he saw the loneliness of things and he saw how much things need love. But he saw yet more than all this. I do not know what he saw, but I know that if we saw it, we too would look sad."

Then the animals began to consider what could be done to make the baby smile.

Almost everyone had an idea.

The cat said she knew an old woman who lived in a cave under a hill who had a magic remedy for almost anything. She stewed the hair from the beard of a billy goat and the tail of a dog in the juice of strange and secret herbs gathered in the dark of the moon. The others said no to this at once.

A sparrow said that he had overheard an angel telling of a potion that was used on cherubs who were out of sorts.

In this potion, the twinkle of a star was poured into the shimmer of a rainbow, and a pink cloud was melted into the sound that lingers in the mind when a song is ended. Then a new thought was allowed to bubble up through the sweetness of an old memory till it frothed. All these were stirred together with sunlight skimmed off before the sun rises and moonlight sifted through a mist. This mixture was said to lift the spirits of any spirit. But the animals decided the ingredients would be too hard to obtain.

It was the white hen who came up with the idea the animals liked best.

"This is a king," she said, "and he needs to be treated like a king. No one has given him any kingly gifts. Naturally he misses these. Let us give him some kingly gifts."

"Do we have any?" asked a guinea fowl.

"I don't know whether *we* do, but *I* certainly do," said the white hen, looking at the guinea fowl with contempt. "I will lay him a clutch of my very best eggs, smooth as porcelain, white as alabaster. They will be like no eggs ever seen before; for whoever eats them will never be hungry again. He will have only to think of them and he will feel fed."

Immediately all the other animals began to think about the kingly gifts they had to give.

"I," said the cow, "will give him my milk, purer than water, better than wine. I will eat only the sweetest hay and freshest clover, and I will chew a sprig of mignonette to give it flavor. It will be like no drink ever drunk before; for when anyone drinks it, he will quench not only his body's thirst but the thirsts of his mind, and he will always feel content."

"I will give him a song," said the pigeon. "It will be a lullaby,

lighter than a summer wind, softer than his mother's breath. And it will have this power: whoever hears it, however troubled of spirit he may be, will instantly fall asleep."

All the other animals had kingly gifts to give, too. The sheep gave her wool to make a blanket that would not only wrap the baby away from the cold air, but from all the world's cares. The donkey gave his back. "Whoever mounts on my back," said the donkey, "will be borne not only to unknown places but to unknowable thoughts." The dog gave his fierce courage; the swallow gave her power to fly above all earthly trouble; the turtle gave his slow patience; the ox gave his brute strength; even the mouse gave a gift—his power to find a hiding place where there was none. "For the day may come," said the mouse, "when he has nowhere to lay his head."

The little pig, of course, gave nothing; the dog would not let him through the fence.

Once he said to the dog, "If only you would let me see him, perhaps I could make him happy."

At this the dog snorted loudly: "If you ask me, it's thinking about pigs and what a problem they are that's making him sad."

The little pig said no more to the dog, but he tried to imagine what gift he might give. He wanted so much to make the little king happy.

He might be like a nightingale, he thought, and sing melodious songs. That should please the little king. But when he opened his mouth to try, the grunts and snorts that issued forth convinced him this was not the gift he had to give.

Then he thought he might be like a bear and put on a fierce show by wrestling with the dog. The mere thought of wrestling with the dog delighted him so much that he felt sure it would make the little king shout aloud with joy. But just then the dog trotted up and barked at him, and he knew he would never have the courage to do that.

Then he decided he might be like a porpoise and dive into the pond in the stable yard, balancing a ball on his nose and leaping through a ring of fire. That would thrill anyone. But when he looked at the pond, he realized that he could not swim and, in fact, did not even like water.

"I'm just an ordinary little pig," he said sadly to himself. Try as he would, he could think of no great and kingly gift he had to give.

But as he sat there, thinking his hardest, his thoughts were interrupted. The swallow came swooping out of the sky, turning somersaults in the air. "Great news! Great news!" she cried for everyone to hear. "My cousin has flown down from the court of Herod the king. Three kings out of the East have been there, looking for the babe. They have seen the star and followed it; and tonight they will be here to worship him, bearing many costly gifts."

When they heard this, all the animals rejoiced; they were sure that three kings out of the East would know what to do to make the baby who was to be a king happy.

It was long after dark when the three kings came. The little pig gazed at them in awe, and so did all the other animals. They were beyond a doubt the most important looking personages that had ever appeared in the stable yard.

The first king was pale of skin, ruddy-cheeked, and beardless. He had blue eyes—the blue of steel rather than of sky—and long golden hair that waved like wheat around his shoulders. He bore a sword the color of his eyes. He wore a golden crown, spiked with sapphires and diamonds. Over his suit of flashing golden mail, his ermine robe fell like wind-blown snow. He rode a white stallion. Fire flashed from its hooves when it pranced and stars sparkled in its mane when it tossed its head.

The second king had skin the color of gold leaf that has aged through many kinds of weather. His slanted eyes were green. A long, thin, black mustache curled down over his lips. His straight black hair fitted his head like a helmet. He brandished a green-gold ax. His crown was green-gold, too, cleft like a bishop's and surmounted by a figure cut from an emerald. His suit was many-colored, all of silk, embroidered with fantastic figures, and over it hung a cape of damask purple. He rode a red-brown camel, tall and double-humped. When the camel breathed, blue smoke curled from its nostrils.

Black of skin was the third king. His eyes were black, deep as still pools of night and dark as dreamless slumber; but they flashed like onyx when the light fell on them. His hair was black, like cropped wool twisted tight against his skull. His beard was black; combed stiff, it thrust forth from his chin. He carried a black spear tipped with a sliver of obsidian. His crown was a plain gold circlet. He wore no undergarment save a black breechcloth. Over it, folded loosely round him, hung a coarse cotton robe, like a monk's. It was red, a dark deep crimson red. He was mounted on a huge elephant, almost as black as himself. When the elephant set down his foot, the earth shook.

The three kings dismounted and went at once into the stable. The animals, who had been gazing at them wide-mouthed and eyes agape as if they had been stricken by a spell, gave a gasp of admiration and poured into the stable behind them. Birds, beasts, barnyard fowl—they had no thought save for the kings. The three claimed every eye.

So it was that the little pig was left unguarded. He needed only a moment. In less time than that, he had wriggled under the fence, shot across the yard, slipped into the stable, and was hiding under a pile of hay in the farthest corner. There he watched.

The three kings marched forward till they came where the young child lay, alone with his mother. For a moment they gazed at him in silence.

Then the first king fell on his knee.

"I am Caspar," said the king, and his voice was like a golden trumpet. "O king most mighty, I have come to bring you my gift."

He opened the lid of the golden casket he carried and, stretching out his hands, set it before the child. It was crammed with golden coins. The gold shone with a rich, soft light that reflected from everything until the whole place shone, as if it were a king's court.

The second king, falling on his knee, said: "I am Melchior," and his voice tinkled like a wind harp. "Here, O king of righteousness, is the gift I have brought."

He set before the child a casket made of jade, with walls so thin it looked as if it had been spun out of green light. When he opened the lid, green tears of frankincense spilled forth and fell upon the ground, and the stable was filled with the fragrance of holiness as if it were a splendid temple.

"I am Balthazar," said the third king, and his voice was soft as the voice in a dream, soft as the hum of bees on a petaled afternoon. "This, Lord, is my gift."

Falling on his knees, he set down before the child his casket, which was carved from one gigantic blood-red ruby. When he opened the lid, the animals saw that it was filled with myrrh. The pieces of myrrh, red and dark, looked like drops of dried blood. Their strong scent filled the air like smoke—a magic smoke, for in it the stable disappeared, and for a moment each animal felt that he was standing alone on a bare hill.

Afterwards, when they discussed this strange vision, most of the animals said they saw three trees on the hill. A few said they saw not trees, but crosses. But the others convinced these that they must have seen myrrh trees and taken them for crosses, since the myrrh is a tree of thorns. For what would crosses have to do with the baby who was to be a king?

The vision lasted only for a moment. Then there they were in the stable again with the three kings kneeling beside their gifts.

They were kingly gifts! The animals all agreed to that. Even the kingliest of kings would have found them worthy to be placed among his treasures.

The baby looked at the gifts, his eyes flickering from gift to gift, almost as if he weighed each one. But his expression did not change. His eyes looked very kind, but they looked sad.

Slowly the three kings rose to their feet and began to back out of the stable. When they rose and backed away, the animals rose and backed away, too, like the little creatures that run up a sandy beach before a great wave. Pell-mell, they all rushed out into the stable yard. They ran out partly because they were impelled by fear and awe, but even more because they were drawn by curiosity. They all wanted to watch the kings ride away on their strange mounts.

In two minutes, nobody was left in the stable but the child and the mother—and the little pig. The little pig had not run out with the others because he was afraid of what they might do if they saw him, and also because he did not want to go. At last he had gotten in to see the baby who was to be a king.

The baby lay in the manger. Spread before him were the golden chest filled with golden coins, and the jade chest filled with tears of frankincense, and the ruby chest filled with pieces of myrrh. But the baby's eyes still looked sad.

The little pig looked at the rich gifts and he felt sad, too; for he knew that he had no such gifts to give. He was only a little pig, alone and frightened.

But suddenly the little pig found himself reaching out of his own helplessness and littleness and sadness, into and through the sadness of the baby. And he knew why the child had never smiled. For he saw that the baby could not be a king until the king had been a baby.

"It has been all wrong," he cried. "The star, and all those angels, and these kings out of the East, and shepherds from the hills, and the inn's people, and all us animals—oh, all of us friendly and with the best intentions!—but what a ruckus and to-do we have made! It has been like a circus!"

The little pig was so carried away by all this that the force of his thoughts pushed him out of the hay where he was hiding.

"Yes, it's been all wrong," he cried again. "These things are what it takes to make a king smile, but not a baby. Can't you see?"

He began to run toward the mother and the baby.

"Only his mother can make her baby smile," he cried, looking up at her.

"If only I could talk to her," he thought. He knew that animals like himself—though they can talk well enough to one another—can hardly ever talk to human beings. But he talked as best he could.

"I could tell you what would make your baby smile," he said to the mother. "For I know what has made babies smile from the beginning of babies. My mother told me!" He said this in the only way he knew how to say it, which was in a little pig's way.

As he ran across the floor, his thoughts stirred him so that his little barrel of a body bounced and bobbed and jiggled and jogged like butter in a churn. One ear went up, one ear went down. His little pink nose wiggled and his little pink tail wiggled, and he made little grunts and snorts that were not at all like a nightingale's song, but formed a happy sound.

And when the young mother saw the little pig running toward her, so pink and roly-poly, jiggling like a jollity, she could not help laughing. She lifted up her son in her arms and she held him out toward the little pig, and she said in a voice so bubbling with laughter that it felt like butterflies: "Look! Look at the little piggie! Oh, what a funny little, happy little fellow!"

As the young mother, laughing, held the baby out to look at him, the little pig saw the sadness starting to go out of the baby's eyes. Then he bounced and jiggled even more in his effort to say what he was saying.

Suddenly the mother drew her son against her breast and held him to her heart. For as she laughed at the pig, an old rhyme had come flashing into her mind, a rhyme she had not heard since she was a baby.

She reached down and touched her son's foot and tickled each one of his toes in turn, and she said:

This little pig went to market,
And this little pig stayed home;
This little pig had roast beef to eat,
And this little pig had none;
This little pig went, "Wee, wee, wee!"
All the way home.

As she spoke the last line, her fingers flashed over her son's form, clear to his mouth, tickling him all the way.

And at that moment some of the cold that circles the world melted, and some of the pain and loneliness that circle living beings melted, too, for when her hand reached his mouth, the baby smiled.

Yes, the baby who was to be a king smiled.

He smiled a baby's smile. That is a wonderful and mysterious event, like spring's buds and morning's light. It is a fragrance blown to us from a small rose—and what garden the rose grew in no one can remember—but we breathe it and we smile.

(For I know that his mother was smiling; a mother always smiles when she sees that her baby is smiling.)

And the little pig—who was the only other living creature there, unless perhaps a mouse had crept back into the stable to keep from being trampled by the crowd outside—I feel certain he smiled, too, and some of the cold and pain and loneliness melted from around his heart.

The last seen of him that night was his little corkscrew tail as it slipped back under the fence; but everyone who saw it agreed that it was wriggling as if it were a smile.

I hope so, for he has made me smile for a moment.

And I pray that you—whatever you may count yourself to be, animal or angel or something in between, and wherever you may find yourself this Christmas, alone or in the company of us in the stable yard—I pray that you may be smiling, too.

THE SNOW—one of those snows where each flake was so big you could not believe in it—should have made it seem like Christmas Eve. But it did not. Perhaps this was because it was twilight. In the city, twilight is a time of day—or is it night?—when it is neither dark nor light, a kind of limbo-ment when the world is not spewed out or swallowed up. This is especially so in winter, when the street lights never seem to be turned on early enough and objects melt into a gray obscurity.

The twilight alone, or the snow alone, would have made for unreality. Together they turned the city into a shapeless, timeless world where everything definite, familiar, usual, dependable was swept away.

It was almost as if God had gone to His window, looked out, and drawn the curtains, but had not yet turned on the lights.

Through this vague void of snow and twilight walked a boy. It did not matter to the boy that every familiar aspect of the street had disappeared; he knew the street as much by his muscles as by sight or sound. He walked up and down it every day, usually several times a day, and he ran up and down it many times more. He lived on the street—in the middle of the next block—and he was on his way home. To get there he simply followed his feet and they followed one another in a pattern they had learned perfectly, the way a pianist's fingers have learned to pick out a piece of music on a keyboard.

The boy always let his feet take him up and down the street. That way he could let his mind take him somewhere else. And usually it did.

While he was walking down the street, he was also finding his way across an impassable desert, climbing an unclimbable mountain, winning the 5,000-meter run at the Olympics or the 500-mile Memorial Day grind at Indianapolis, running the length of the field for a touchdown in the Superbowl, hitting a home run in the World Series.

Today, in the snow, he was beating up his brothers. This was a favorite pastime—in his mind, that is. In the flesh, they usually beat him up. They were older, bigger, and stronger.

It was always him against them. At least that is the way it seemed to him.

His brothers were not only bigger and stronger, but different—and alike in their difference. They played together, exchanged thoughts together, and often ran off together and left him. So he tried to come at them unawares; he would pounce on them unexpectedly, trip them when they were not looking, leap on their backs.

This usually brought him a pummeling. It brought his father's wrath down on him, too. The boy was very proud of his father. His father was a jet pilot, in the Air Force. But he did not think his father was very proud of him.

When his father came on them fighting, he was the one his father grabbed and swatted. "Leave them alone," his father would say to him. "I've told you a thousand times."

His father never swatted his brothers. They were perfect—like his father. Perfectly big, perfectly strong, perfectly smart—perfectly unlike him.

He often heard his father bragging about them to friends.

"Quentin has never made any grade but A," he would say, or, "Evan has such a high IQ his teachers say he is in the genius class."

When his father was talking to friends about *him*, he was usually saying, "I don't know what gets into that boy!"

At least, that is the way it seemed to him.

He was not big. He was not strong. He was not smart. He did not like school. Not because it was hard; it was easy. But it was dull. He would rather watch TV, or read a book, or dream, or think, or play by himself. When he was not dogging his brothers, he played by himself. His favorite playthings were marbles. He had two cigar boxes full of them. He never played the game of marbles, but for hours playing with the marbles on the rug, he ran sports events, fought battles, dueled, held parades, and organized revolutions.

This Christmas Eve he was walking home after playing football with his brothers. Having kicked off his tennis shoes, he had played in his stocking feet, and when he put his shoes back on, they were full of snow; but he had played on, shaking with cold, bedraggled, his clothes soaking wet, his teeth chattering until his older brother had ordered him to go home. In reply he had jumped on his brother's back and had been hurled into the snow.

While his older brother held him, his other brother twisted his arm until he promised he would go home. Then they let him up and immediately ran away, shouting what they would do to him if he did not keep his promise.

So as he walked down the street, he was beating up his brothers in his mind.

By the time he reached the street corner nearest his house, he had mentally reduced them to the condition where they came crawling on their knees to beg him for mercy.

And just at this point, unexpectedly, his fantasy changed. Someone in one of the houses along the street must have opened a door, for out upon the air poured the sound of a Christmas carol; it was only a few notes—whoever opened the door must have shut it immediately—but suddenly the boy, almost to his consternation, instead of kicking his brothers as they knelt, was holding out his hands to them—and in his hands were gifts. In one hand he held two Indian chiefs made out of lead, and in the other a penknife. The remarkable thing about these gifts was that of all the things he owned, he esteemed these most. The Indians were a gift from his father. He had many lead Indians, but these two were special; you had only to glance at them to see that they were superior. His brother Evan had always wanted them and had tried to trade him out of them.

His father had given the knife to him, too, and like the Indians it was superior. It contained two blades, a punch, a screwdriver, a can-opener, a bottle-opener, and a nail file. "That's a fine German knife," his father had told him, "the best in the world!" Not even his older brother had such a knife, and Quentin had wanted it very much.

Now, just as he was about to step off the curb, he paused in his mind and instead of beating his brothers, held out to them these two possessions that were dearest to him in this world.

For a moment, the deep attachment that he felt for his brothers, the fierce longing to be one with them, came welling up in him so overwhelmingly that it brought him to a halt, half-suspended on the curbstone.

As he paused, through the snow and semi-dark a car came spinning. Out of control, it made a complete circle and slid sideways directly toward him. A wheel smashed into the curb where he stood; the car bounced, skidded, tipped, righted itself, shot back into the street, and hurtled past.

The boy had involuntarily thrown up his arms. The car was so close he felt it touch a hand, but it merely brushed against his fingers lightly, like a wing, and flashed away.

Everything happened so quickly that the boy had had time neither to move nor speak. Now, as the car disappeared, he waved his fists and shouted after it: "You crazy nut! You crazy nut!"

Then he stood shaking and muttering, not certain whether he was more frightened or outraged.

"You crazy nut!" he shouted once more. But the car had vanished as quickly as it had materialized. The twilight snow filled everything in every direction; even the marks the car had made in the street were already beginning to be obliterated.

The boy started across the street again. But this time, first he looked both ways.

This is how he happened to see it.

Something was lying in the middle of the intersection. The boy ran toward it. It's a woman, he thought. That crazy nut hit her!

Then he stopped short.

It was not a woman.

It was not easy to see just what it was, but he clearly saw bare feet sticking out from under a white robe and then he saw . . . wings.

Wings! The thing had wings! It's a spaceman, he thought. For a moment he considered running. But only for a moment. If it *was* a spaceman, it was unconscious. Slowly he walked nearer to it. And suddenly he knew what it was. He had seen many pictures—and it was exactly like the pictures.

This was an angel.

The only thing surprising about it was its size. It was huge!

A white robe with a strange fringe hung loosely over the massive body. The boy's eyes took in the bare feet and legs, the burly arms, the huge hands, the gentle face—the eyes were closed—the tousled curly hair, but it was none of these that he really looked at. He looked at the wings. Though he had never seen anyone as big and powerful looking as this angel, not even in a pro football game on TV, he had seen big and powerful men. But he had never, never at all, seen anyone with wings.

The wings were great white feathered things. One of them lay folded at its side, but the other was twisted almost at right angles to the angel's body.

The boy could see in a moment why the angel lay there.

The angel had a broken wing.

His first impulse was to run home for help, but then he realized he could not just leave the angel lying in the middle of the street in the snow.

He looked around, but he saw no one else.

"Help! Help!" he shouted, but no answer came.

It was clearly up to him to get the angel out of the street. Almost without thinking, he reached under the angel's shoulders and with all his power, heaved the huge form from the ground—and almost fell over. The angel came up in his arms as if it weighed nothing at all. *The angel weighed nothing at all!* The boy ran with him to the sidewalk and stood for a moment holding in his arms this great lolling burden that weighed nothing at all. As he carried it down the street toward his house, he kept looking at it in astonishment.

The figure was huge. It sprawled out of his arms. And it was solidly firm. The boy had once shaken hands with Muhammad Ali, but he had never felt such a sense of sheer muscular power as he felt now. Yet the angel was weightless.

It worried the boy, too, that the angel was so big that its broken wing, which hung askew, kept dragging in the street and bumping against things; for from time to time the angel winced, though it did not regain consciousness.

When he got the door of his house open, the boy paused. "Hey!" he called. "Hey!" There was no one home. He carried the angel to his own room and laid it down in his bed. It overflowed the bed. Then carefully, oh so carefully, he lifted the broken wing and placed it in the position that he felt it should have. As he did so, he felt a vast, almost electrical surge that caused his fingers to tingle and his body to glow, but the angel did not move.

The boy sat and watched it. After a while, he became aware that he still had on his wet clothes. He did not feel cold at all. This was strange, because he had been shivering before he met the angel and usually just being alone in the house made him feel lonely and cold, even when he was warm. Now, even when he was cold, he felt warm. He pulled off his soaking tennis shoes and socks, went into the bathroom for a towel, came back, and began to put on dry clothes.

He had just finished dressing when he had a sense that he was being watched. He looked at the angel. The angel had opened its eyes—or were they eyes? They were looking right at him, right into him, right through him, but they were the most extraordinary eyes he had ever seen. They were not eyes. They were stars. When he looked at them, it was as though he were looking right through space into worlds beyond his own, worlds of light. The light danced and flickered and shone like flame, for it was the light of stars. He could not say what color the eyes were. At times it was like looking into a day sky and at times it was like looking into a night sky. But always it was like looking through infinites of space, not at eyes but stars. He felt dazzled but at the same time he felt drawn—and he felt peace.

"Thank you," said the angel, "for helping me."

Like its eyes, the angel's voice was strange. The boy was not sure whether the angel spoke or sang. It made the boy think of a choir singing in church on a sunny morning, yet it seemed like speech. Later, when he tried to remember, he was unsure whether he had heard words or thought them.

"A car ran over you," said the boy.

"No," said the angel.

"It almost ran over me," said the boy.

"Yes," said the angel.

The boy and the angel looked at each other.

"Would you like a drink of water?" said the boy.

The angel shook its head.

"A peanut butter sandwich?" said the boy.

"No," said the angel.

The angel reached up and with a grimace pulled its wing more firmly into place. It sighed.

"I—I didn't know what to do about the wing," said the boy. "I hope I didn't hurt you."

"You did beautifully," said the angel. "The wing will be all right. We angels mend fast. A few hours and I will be like new."

"I never thought angels. . . ." The boy stopped.

"Angels usually do not have accidents," said the angel, completing his thought. "It was clumsy of me. Too little visibility and too much speed."

The boy thought he heard bells tinkling—many bells, gold and silver and bronze and crystal bells. Then he realized he was hearing the angel laughing.

The angel shut its eyes and lay still. When it opened them again, it said, "Your name is . . . ?"

"Johnnie," said the boy. "Do you have a name?"

"Of course," said the angel. "You can call me Mort."

"Mort? That doesn't sound like an angel's name."

"Oh, but it is. A very old one," said the angel.

The boy laughed. "Hi, Mort!"

"Hi, Johnnie," said the angel.

"I wish my brothers were here," said the boy. "Wait'll they see you."

"Oh, yes, your brothers—you were playing with them just before you found me," said the angel.

"Yeah, football."

"Oh, I thought you had been beating them up," said the angel.

"Beating them up?" said the boy.

"You had them crawling on their knees, as I remember," said the angel.

"Oh, that was only in my mind," said the boy.

"Only in your mind?" said the angel.

"Sure. I didn't really beat them up—I just wanted to," he said.

"That's better?" said the angel.

The boy felt a sudden stab of fear. "Look, if you came because I'd like to beat my brothers up, they're always beating me up. What about that?"

The angel did not answer.

"You think I don't like my brothers, don't you? Is that why you're here?" The thought shot through the boy's mind that tomorrow was Christmas. Perhaps God was checking up on him.

"No," said the angel, "I am here because you *do* like them. In fact, you love them. That is how I broke my wing. At the last moment, my feet caught in your love."

The boy laughed. "Your feet caught in my love? That's a funny thing."

"Love is a very real thing—as you can see." The angel looked wryly at his wing. "We angels are always falling over love—or hate. Just like people."

The boy looked at him as if he did not quite understand.

"But to return to your brothers," the angel went on, "you had beaten them soundly. They were on their knees."

"I'd given them my karate chop," said the boy.

"You know karate?" said the angel.

"Sure. Judo, too; I watch TV."

"But having driven them to their knees, you stopped beating them," said the angel.

"Maybe," said the boy.

"Yes, you held out your hands to them, not in anger, but offering gifts."

The boy said nothing.

"Two Indians and a penknife," said the angel.

The boy ran to the bureau, opened a drawer, and brought out a small box. From it he took two Indians and a penknife and held them out to the angel.

"I see you keep them in a very special place. Do you have other things in the box?"

"Nah. Just personal things."

"Like?" persisted the angel.

The boy looked embarrassed. Finally he drew out a small, dog-eared snapshot. It was of his father, his mother, and his two brothers, much younger than they now were; he himself was not in it.

"And that's all?"

The boy drew forth a battered earring.

The angel looked at it. "It must be precious!"

"Nah. Just a plain old earring."

"Then why do you keep it? Because it was your mother's?"

The boy looked at the angel almost angrily. "If you know everything, what are you asking me for?"

"Forgive me," said the angel. "I should not pry into your private mind. But it is a habit with us angels." The angel had been examining the Indians and the knife. "I see why you like these so much. They are beautiful."

"The best!" said the boy.

"And you were going to give them away!"

"Not really."

"Tomorrow is Christmas. What Christmas presents they would make! Your brothers would love them," said the angel.

"Huh! What'll they give me?" snorted the boy. "Something from the dime store?"

"Do they have things you would like?" asked the angel.

"I'll say. Lots of things. Lots more things than I have. But they never let me touch them," said the boy.

"For instance?" said the angel.

For a moment the boy's eyes gleamed.

"Quent has a baseball autographed by all the St. Louis Cardinals. It was in the World Series."

"That would certainly be a valuable ball," said the angel. "He probably would not give it to you. Still, your knife and Indians would make beautiful Christmas presents—unexpected ones, too. Those are the best kind, are they not?"

The boy laid his possessions on the table and said, "You'd like me to give these to them, wouldn't you?"

"I would like you to do what you would like to do. That is all," said the angel.

"Do you give things to people?" said the boy.

"Sometimes," said the angel.

"I suppose when you want to give somebody something, you just make a wish and there it is—just like that," said the boy.

"Sometimes," said the angel.

"You really can?" said the boy.

The angel nodded its head.

"Could you for me?" said the boy.

"What would you like me to do?" said the angel.

"Get me that baseball."

The boy had no sooner spoken the words than he held a baseball in his hand. He turned it over.

"Do you really want your brother's baseball?" said the angel.

The boy stood gazing at the ball. Then he looked at the angel. Then he looked at the ball. Then his face clouded with indecision. And a strange thing happened to the ball. The ball began to disappear, not all at once as it had come, but pulsing into view and out again; then slowly, almost as if reluctantly, it vanished.

"It's gone!" the boy exclaimed.

"You wished it to go," said the angel.

"You really can work magic." The boy looked admiringly at the angel. "You made Quent's old ball appear and disappear just like that. I bet you could make this whole house disappear."

"Please do not wish that," said the angel. "We would be out in the snow. You would not be comfortable."

"I bet you could make the whole world disappear," said the boy.

"I will not be called on to do that tonight, I hope," said the angel.

"I bet you could make anything you wanted to happen!"

"There are limits," said the angel.

"If I wanted something else beside Quent's old ball, could you give me that?" said the boy.

"Perhaps," said the angel.

"Could you give me anything I wanted?" said the boy.

"I cannot grant every wish, if that is what you mean," said the angel.

"What kind can't you?" asked the boy.

"I cannot make a person do something he would not do. I cannot keep him from doing something he would do. But I can help him to keep from doing what he does not want to do, and I can help him to do what he wants to do—even when he does not know what he wants. Do you have a wish?"

The boy thought about this for a while. Then he said, "I guess I don't truly know what I wish for."

Just then there was a noise in the doorway. His brothers were standing there. "What are you talking to yourself about?" said Quentin.

The boy looked at his brothers. He looked at the angel. His eyes went back and forth between them. "Aren't you surprised?" he said at last.

"Surprised?" said Quentin.

The boy pointed at the angel. "At him!"

The brothers looked where he pointed. "Him? Who?" said Evan.

"The angel!"

"What did you say?" said Quentin.

"The angel with the broken wing!"

Quentin and Evan drew back. "Angel with a broken wing?"

"Sure. There in the bed," said the boy.

His brothers' eyes flicked toward the bed, then back at him.

"Don't they see you?" the boy asked the angel.

"Is he nuts?" Evan said.

Quentin winked at Evan. "It's another one of those crazy games he's always playing in his head. You know. Soldiers. Or knights. Now it's angels." Then he looked at the bed.

"Sure I see him. I see him and I'm going to catch him before he gets away." Suddenly, quickly, he dived toward the bed.

But for once his small brother was even quicker. As Quentin lunged, the smaller boy ducked under him and rising, caught him with one shoulder to catapult him like a projectile. Quentin sprawled on the floor. Red-faced, he rose to his hands and knees. "The rug slipped," he said.

The boy turned toward the angel. "Don't they see you?"

"I should have warned you," said the angel. "Hardly anyone ever does."

"Say something to them," said the boy.

"I do not think they are in a mood to listen," said the angel.

"Sure he says something to us," said Quentin. "He says you are a nut." Then he nodded at Evan.

The two propelled themselves from opposite sides onto their brother. But just as they flung themselves together, the small boy slipped from beneath their grasp and they crashed into one another, their heads colliding with a loud thump. Both let out a cry of pain and dropped to the floor. For a few moments neither tried to rise. They sat rubbing their heads where knots were beginning to form. At last Quentin hissed at Evan, "Why didn't you watch where you were going?"

Then their father's voice came up the stairwell. "Come to dinner, boys." Johnnie had not known his father was home.

Quentin got back onto his feet. He was still holding his head and staring angrily at everybody—Evan, Johnnie, and the bed. "You've played these crazy games so long," he said at last, "you're crazy. You think you see an angel with a broken wing. I see a brother with a broken brain. You get that? You've got a broken brain." He rubbed his own head. "And you're gonna have worse than that. C'mon, Evan." The two boys left the room.

Johnnie looked at the angel with dismay and doubt, but the latter merely said, "You do know judo."

"Was that judo?" asked the boy, still breathing hard.

"A perfect performance," said the angel.

"I think you helped," said the boy.

"I guided a little, perhaps," said the angel. "But the truth is they did it to themselves, a case of force reaching beyond itself."

"They didn't see you," said the boy.

"No," said the angel.

"But my dad—he'll see you!"

"He probably will not," said the angel. "I would not advise telling him yet."

"You aren't just in my mind, are you?" said the boy.

"What is just in your mind? What is out of your mind?" asked the angel.

The boy sat and knitted his brows, wrestling with his thoughts.

"I am as real," said the angel, "as anything in this room. As real as Quentin or Evan. As real as you. Is that real enough?"

The boy did not answer.

"Come here," said the angel.

The boy walked to the bed.

"Take my hand," said the angel, and grasped the boy's hand in his own. Again the boy had that sense of indescribable firmness and strength he had had when he carried the angel. The hand was nothing, nothing at all. Yet the boy knew that he had taken hold of the most real thing he had ever felt. It was so real it made him feel more real—stronger and firmer inside himself.

"You had better go eat your dinner," said the angel.

After dinner, his father turned to him.

"Your brothers have been telling me you have an angel in your room."

The boy looked at his brothers. They were grinning.

The boy said nothing.

"Well?" said his father.

"How would they know?" said the boy.

"Yes, how would they? Did you see him, boys?"

"No," said Evan. "Johnnie said he's there."

"Did you tell them there's an angel in your room?" asked the father.

Johnnie nodded.

"This is a game, of course," said his father.

The boy said nothing.

"Well?"

Still the boy said nothing.

"I guess we should go see." His father took him by the hand and started toward his room. Quentin and Evan started after them. "You can stay, boys," said their father. The brothers stopped.

The angel was still lying on the bed. The boy thought he was asleep.

"Now just where is this angel?" asked the father.

"You don't see him?" asked the boy sadly.

"I certainly don't," said the father.

"He said you probably wouldn't." The boy pointed to the bed.

"In the bed, is he? Let's see." The father walked toward the bed and was about to thrust his hands into the bed clothes when suddenly he choked and began to cough. He straightened, struggling for breath, but the coughing fit would not stop. The boy ran to the bathroom and returned with a glass of water. The father sat down in the chair and drank it slowly. At last he could breathe freely again. He looked at the bed thoughtfully.

"Come here, son," he said, and took the boy on his knees.

"Now how did this angel get here?"

The boy told him how the car had come skidding out of the snow, brushed against him, and hurtled on, and when he had looked up, there the angel lay in the street, with a broken wing.

"You carried him home?" said his father.

"Yes. It's the funniest thing. He's big, but he doesn't weigh anything at all."

"Of course not," said his father. "Wouldn't this indicate he isn't really there?"

"But he *is* there," said the boy, turning to the angel. "Mort, can't you let him see?" The angel only smiled.

"Mort?" said his father. "What is Mort?"

"Mort is his name," said the boy.

"You named him that?"

"No, no. He told me his name," said the boy.

The father stared at the boy and drew him closer. He looked again at the bed, more sharply and apprehensively than before.

"You're a very imaginative boy," he said. "But it's time now to stop this."

The boy said nothing.

"You are making it up!"

The boy said nothing.

"Look! Nobody but you can see this angel."

The boy said nothing.

"Nobody but you can hear this angel."

The boy looked at his father. His father was frowning and beginning to look angry. The boy looked at the angel. The angel was smiling and continuing to look peaceful.

"Mort!" cried the boy suddenly.

The father rose from the chair and seized him by the shoulder, "Stop it!"

"Mort, Mort!" the boy cried again. "Speak to him. Let him see you, please."

The father shook the boy hard. "There is no angel, do you understand? No angel!" He was shouting. "If you have to play games, can't you play a happy game? Tomorrow is Christmas."

"But it is a happy game," said the boy. "Mort is a very happy angel."

The father gripped the boy's shoulder so tightly that it hurt.

"There is no angel."

The boy shook his head.

"You are not to speak of him again," commanded his father. "This is a direct order."

But the boy continued shaking his head. "There is an angel, there is an angel."

His father raised his hand. But before he could bring it down, the angel reached out its hand and touched him on the shoulder joint. Immediately the arm stiffened and fell rigid at his side. His father grasped it with his other hand and began to rub it wildly.

"What's the matter?" said the boy.

"My arm has a terrible cramp," said the man, his face contorted. Then, suddenly, the arm was normal again. The man heaved a great sigh. Still rubbing his arm, he walked to the door. He stared for a moment at the bed. "I'll be back," he said in a fierce voice and went out.

"You hurt him," the boy said to the angel.

"He felt the touch of a reality beyond his power to bear, that is all," said the angel. "And not for long. I could touch him only because he really did not want to strike you."

"He seemed to want to," said the boy, his eyes full of tears.

"But he did not want to, any more than you wanted me to hurt him. You were angry with me when I did."

"I just wish they could see you. Then things would be different. Why can't they see you?"

"You see me," said the angel.

"Won't they ever see you?" persisted the boy.

"Someday."

"All of them?"

"All of them."

"Will you stay here till they do?" asked the boy.

"My wing will be healed by morning. I shall go then," said the angel.

"I'll be sorry to see you go," said the boy.

"Will you?" said the angel. "I am afraid I have just complicated things for you with your family. And here it is Christmas."

"I know," said the boy. "Do you have Christmas?"

"Every day," said the angel.

"Christmas every day! That must be great."

"It keeps us busy. There is a great deal to do," said the angel.

"Do you get presents?"

"Continually," said the angel, "and give them, too."

Suddenly the boy glanced at the Indians and the penknife that still lay on the table by the bed. He took out two pieces of paper and slowly printed: "For Quentin." "For Evan." One piece he wrapped around the Indians, and the other around the knife, and fastened them with rubber bands.

"I'm going to give them to them," he said.

"I thought you would," said the angel. "You probably will not get the ball, you know."

"That's all right," said the boy. "They're my brothers."

"So they are." The angel looked at the boy for a long time, a look filled with affection and admiration and apprehension. "All human beings are looking for a way to be brothers, do you know that?"

"Yes, I know," said the boy.

"Perhaps you are the one to work out the way," said the angel.
"Me?" said the boy.
"Somebody has to. Why should it not be you?" said the angel.
"It's very important, isn't it?" said the boy.
"The most important thing in the world."
"Like winning a war?"
"It *is* winning the war," said the angel. "Every other war will be lost if you lose this one—even if you win them. Every other war will be won if you win this one—even if you lose them. Do you understand what I am saying?"
"Not exactly," said the boy, "but you mean you want me to try and be a brother to my brothers."
"Yes, and to show others how," said the angel.
"I don't know how," said the boy.
"You did it," said the angel, pointing to the two little packages.
"Yes," said the boy, "but I'm not sure how. It was like working a puzzle and you don't know how you worked it. You just did it. Then you have to figure out how."
"You did it; you can do it again," said the angel. "It will be even easier next time. And you will get it clear, all worked out."
"I don't know," said the boy. "That might take a long time."
"It might," said the angel.
"I'd better go down and slip these presents under the Christmas tree," said the boy, "so they'll be there in the morning."
When he came back, the angel was sitting on the edge of the bed, so he sat down in the chair. The angel's starry eyes were flashing, and the boy felt himself drawn into them and wandering through their depths. His head began to nod.
Suddenly he sat up. "If I fall asleep, you won't just leave without waking me, will you?"
"We had better say good-bye now," said the angel. "My strength has almost returned."
"Will you ever come back?" asked the boy.
"I will be back."
"Soon?"
"I will be back. If you ever want me enough, you have a wish I have not granted. Never be afraid to wish."
"I'll remember," said the boy. Again his head began to nod. Once he jerked himself awake. Then his head fell forward again.

"Good night," said the angel in a voice so soft it seemed almost the whisper of the snow falling outside the window, only it had a warm sound.

But the boy was asleep.

The angel lifted him gently from the chair and laid him in the bed. It drew the covers over him and for a long time sat watching him. The hours raced toward morning.

Then the father was standing in the doorway, looking into the room. He saw the boy asleep in the bed and sighed with relief. The boy was in the bed; that meant it had been a game; there was no angel. He tiptoed to the bed and adjusted the bedcovers.

But as he bent over his sleeping son, his apprehension returned, for his sense of a presence in the room began to grow again. It was the same sense he sometimes had had in combat—when he felt an enemy plane before he saw it.

Then he looked up and saw the angel clear. It was standing looking out of the window. As the father looked at the angel, the angel turned and looked at the father.

The angel did not say anything, but the stars that were his eyes shone brilliantly, and the man knew that he was gazing into unfathomable depths.

"I felt you knew I was here," said the angel.

"I didn't. Not at first," said the father. "Since you touched my arm, I have been trying not to believe in you."

"I was sure you would see me," said the angel. "You are a soldier, are you not?"

"A bomber pilot, yes."

"You are a lot like Johnnie," said the angel.

"I suppose so," said the father.

"Is that why you whip him sometimes?" asked the angel. "And not the others?"

"I—I don't know."

"We are close. You and I," said the angel. "You thought if you acted certain, Johnnie would begin to disbelieve in me." The angel looked gently at the sleeping boy.

"Do not awaken him," said the father quickly. "He must not know I saw you."

"He will not awaken," said the angel.

A sudden look of fright crossed the father's face.

"I do not mean he will *never* awaken," said the angel quickly. "You know who I am, of course."

"Of course," said the father. "As you say, I'm a soldier. And that name you gave Johnnie. It could only be one angel."

"I thought you would recognize it."

"*Mort.* The French word for death. Of course, I recognized it. And why should I not know you? You took my wife."

"Yes. I remember. When Johnnie was born." The angel shut its eyes and it was suddenly as if all the lights went out. The stars were there, but now they were dark. And the man was staring into dark worlds of mysteries, too deep for him to plumb and understand. Then the angel opened his eyes, and again the room was filled with soft light.

"Why did you come here?" said the father.

"I was on an errand," said the angel.

"The usual one?" said the father.

"The usual one," said the angel.

"To take someone back with you?" said the father.

The angel nodded.

"Johnnie?" said the father.

The angel fixed his eyes with the father's and again nodded.

The father began to walk rapidly back and forth in the little room. He gazed at his sleeping son. Then he stepped quickly between his son and the angel.

"You can't. He's just a boy," he said.

"Sometimes I have to take boys," said the angel.

"But why?"

"Not even I know that. I am the servant of a higher wisdom. It is in charge."

"Take me instead," cried the father in a hoarse voice.

"Such substitutions are hardly ever approved. The rules are pretty strict about that sort of thing," said the angel.

"But it would make sense," said the father.

"To you, perhaps. But there is a higher sense, a divine reason. It is this that runs the world. Its meaning is not always clear—even to me—but it is there. And it is order."

The father still stood between the angel and his son, half-defiant, half-pleading.

"You love him," said the angel.

"Of course," said the father.
"So much that you would take his place and go with me?"
The man looked at the angel as if he were horrified that it could have any other notion.
"Yet you would have whipped him."
The father said nothing.
"On Christmas Eve," said the angel.
"Yes."
"Because he insisted he saw an angel."
"Yes."
"That you saw too."
"I hadn't seen you then."
"All right. That you felt might be there."
The man nodded.
"But why? Why?"
"Because I love him."
"Impossible. And yet, of course. You were bewildered. Frightened. So you did the thing you have learned to do. You struck out. It is as when you are leading a squadron. The enemy is nearby. You do not know where. But you know what to do: stay in formation! Johnnie had gotten out of formation. You had to get him back."
"I suppose it's like that," said the father. "I knew Johnnie was in danger. And I did the only thing I knew to do. I applied discipline. Force. I did not know what was wrong, but I knew something was wrong."
"Wrong?" said the angel. "Perhaps it was right. Perhaps it was the rightest thing that ever has happened in your life."
"Right or wrong, I knew something was happening that threatened the way things were—and I had to fight to preserve that way."
"Why?"
The man looked at the angel in surprise and indignation. "Because I'm the father."
"Father, you can be at ease then," said the angel. "You no longer have to guard your son from me."
"But you said you had come to take him."
"I came to take him, but he changed my mind."
"Changed your mind?"
"Yes, the order I serve is not an autocratic one. My Sovereign is no dictator. I, like all my fellows, serve the highest possible purpose, and

the wisdom I serve is always love, however you may view it. We angels are committed to obey the cause of wisdom, but we are free. We can follow another course, if something happens that would indicate another course to be wiser."

"And something happened?" said the father.

"I fell and broke my wing! That does not happen often."

"I've been wondering about that," said the father. "How could an angel break his wing?"

"I ran into an unexpected object—a thought."

"A thought?"

"A thought of love. Johnnie's," said the angel. "As I came down, Johnnie was thinking. It was a small boy's thought of love—but a small boy's thought of love can be unusual—do you not know that?"

"I know," said the father.

"That afternoon Johnnie had been playing football with his brothers. As usual, they had won. So Johnnie had gone off by himself and hated them for a while.

"He told you how he stepped off the curb and the car came speeding around the corner through the snow and half-light. It was just then that he had this thought. He had this thought, and it stopped him, there on the curb, one foot off, one foot on. The car skidded past him, and I ran hard into his thought and it broke my wing."

"What was the thought like?" asked the father.

"That I cannot say exactly. It was vague. Unformed. Unfinished. That is the best word. Unfinished. If he had had it sharp, I could tell you what it was. Then you could have it and I could take Johnnie. It was full of love—and power. So loving and powerful that it prompted him to give his brothers two lead Indians and a penknife."

"His most precious possessions," exclaimed the father.

"He has put them under the tree," said the angel.

The father swallowed hard.

"But the thought that made him do it was not worked out in detail. A small boy's fantasy—little more. Only a step, you understand?"

The father nodded.

"We cannot afford to overlook the least step. It is too important. Man has to learn how to love. He wants to, but he has to learn how. So just on the chance that Johnnie may help him learn how, I have to give him the time."

"You mean Johnnie may be the one to show human beings how to live together?'' said the father.

''I do not know. That depends on Johnnie. Somebody is going to.''

''But Johnnie!''

''Why not Johnnie? Is he not your son?''

The man looked surprised, as though this thought had not occurred to him.

''Everybody is somebody's son—or daughter,'' said the angel. ''The President. The man who invented the atom bomb. Why not the man who learns to control it? The Man whose birthday you are celebrating today was the son of a carpenter, and born in a manger.''

The father looked at his son, who stirred in his sleep and smiled. Head tossed back, smiling, one arm thrown out of the covers, he lay sleeping. He is the most completely natural, normal looking boy I've ever seen, thought the father.

''So he is,'' said the angel, answering his thought. ''Are we not fortunate!''

The father walked to the window. ''It's almost dawn.''

''Yes, and my wing is mended,'' said the angel. ''Angels never suffer long, though sometimes the hurt is very deep.''

''You suffer!'' exclaimed the father. ''It never occurred to me you might suffer. You have caused so many tears.''

''Then would you have me never weep? We angels do not weep often, but when we do, our tears are fire and fall through space. That is one way worlds are formed. On these worlds that once were the tears of angels, life finds its meaning through tears—tears of anguish and tears of longing and tears of compassion. But the meaning that it finds is never a little one.''

Is he trying to tell me the earth is such a world? thought the father; but he did not ask.

''This is Christmas morning,'' said the angel at last. ''Christmas is a family time. My wing is whole. It is time for me to leave.''

''Aren't you going to say good-bye to Johnnie?''

''I have said good-bye,'' said the angel. ''He will remember, but he will remember the way we remember all the most important things—as if they were dreams.''

The angel stepped to the bedside. He put his hand on Johnnie's forehead, and the boy's breathing became so still the father could not be sure he breathed at all.

''Dream,'' said the angel to the sleeping boy. ''Great dreams! In a moment your sleep will end, but your dreams will not end. They will have only begun."

Suddenly, the starry eyes of the angel overflowed and one tear ran down its cheek, but it did not fall through space and form a world. It fell on the boy's forehead. A soft flame flew up and filled the room with light.

The father felt the light and the flame and with it an overwhelming sense of suffering and longing and compassion, and he felt that all the pain and hope and love that God had felt from the beginning of time was in that room. He uttered a strange cry and tears began to flow from his own eyes.

"This will never do," said the angel. "It is Christmas and your family has a right to see you happy. Here, dry your eyes."

He held out the fringe of his robe.

Before he could think, the father had pressed it to his eyes. The moment he did it, he felt a strange joy—the pain and hope and love were not less, but altogether they formed a joy, an overreaching joy compounded out of them, the way a perfume is compounded out of elements that in themselves are not fragrant.

"Good-bye," said the angel. It looked at the boy and smiled. "I've left him a Christmas present, something for a little boy."

Suddenly where the angel stood, there was an explosion of light that flowed outward to fill the room and then rushed backward upon itself and disappeared into itself, draining all the light out of the room. The father felt something brush his cheek, and he had the sense of a wing tip, unimaginably soft and unbelievably powerful. He stared at the spot where the angel had been, and he felt that he was staring into an endless and impossible abyss that drew world upon world into it and yet was empty.

Then everything was exactly as it had been before yesterday, except that now it was today.

The boy sat upright in bed, looking wildly around the room.

"Where is he? Where is he?" he cried. His eyes focused on his father. "Dad, it's you."

"Yes, it's me." He walked to the side of the bed.

"But he's gone!" said the boy.

"Is he?" said the father.

"I—I've been asleep," said the boy.

"You have been asleep," said the father.

“Dreaming?”

“Dreaming!”

Then the eyes of both of them were drawn to what the boy held in his hands. For in his hands he held an angel.

It was perfect, the bare feet, the fringed robe, the powerful body, the tousled head, the gentle face, even the eyes that were not eyes but stars. It was a perfect angel, perfect in every detail—except one wing was broken. It hung twisted by its side.

“It's him,” said the boy.

“It's him,” said the father.

Just then there came a great shout from the hall and a sound of running feet.

“It's Christmas. It's Christmas. Get up. Get up, everybody! Last one down's a baboon.” It was Evan shouting.

The boy looked at his father. The father looked at his son. They reached out, their hands touched, and they went down to the living room. The others were already around the tree.

“Merry Christmas! Merry Christmas!” they shouted.

“What's that Johnnie has?” said his brother Evan. “Why, it's his angel. Let's see that,” and he reached out to take it from his hands.

“No,” said the father. “It's Johnnie's.”

“No,” said the boy, “it's not mine, it's ours. It's our Christmas angel. Lift me up, Dad!” He held out his arms to his father. “To the top of the tree!”

With his father holding him, he fastened the angel to the top of the tree.

For a moment they all stood and gazed at it. The room filled with a strange soft light, a little like love, a little like hope, and a little like suffering, yet altogether a joyous light.

But I do not think anyone there saw anything unusual about the light in the room. If they thought of it at all, they just thought of it as the light of Christmas morning, for their own thoughts were full of light.

Then, with a whoop, they fell to opening their presents.

A Gift from Rosa

WHEN ST. FRANCIS built the first crèche—the stable scene of the birth of Jesus—back in the thirteenth century, people came from everywhere to look at it. Most people in those days knew little about anything, even about such an important event as the birth of Jesus. So when they gathered around the creche, Francis, who was a great storyteller, would tell them many legends and wondertales connected with Christmas.

Francis loved all living things, so his stories were often about birds and beasts.

Here is one of them.

Once upon a time (said St. Francis) there was a little girl named Rosa. She was very poor, so poor that often she didn't have enough to eat and had to go hungry to bed.

What's that? You are feeling sorry for Rosa because she went hungry to bed? I've gone hungry to bed most of my life and I don't think I've missed much except for a few stomachaches.

Rosa had a naturally sunny disposition, and hard as this may be for more fortunate persons like ourselves to understand, most of the time Rosa was happy. When she went down the street, she usually skipped, and when she was alone, she usually sang.

Except for the thin shift she wore to cover her, she had only one small possession.

This was a bird.

It was a small bird, hardly larger than a sparrow and just as undistinguished.

One spring day as she went skipping and singing along, she found it lying in the street. She could see at a glance it was hurt and couldn't fly, so she picked it up.

"Hello, little bird!" she said, and sang a few notes by way of greeting.

The little bird did not sing back. It looked at her with piteous and frightened eyes and huddled in the hollow of her hands as if it wished to hide. She could feel the fluttering of its heart.

Rosa had never held anything so soft and warm and small and helpless. All her life she had felt many needs, but she had never before felt anything that needed her. This bird, she instantly knew, needed her. If she set it back down in the street, it would die.

She carried it home with her.

Rosa was used to making something out of nothing, so in a short time she had woven a little cage of twigs in which her bird could live as snugly as if it were a golden canary in a gilded cage.

The bird was not like a canary; not only was it plain, but its song was no more than a croak. Rosa decided that whatever had affected its flight had also affected its voice.

Rosa did not care what the bird was. She loved it. That was enough. The few crumbs she had, she shared with the bird and she gave it all her heart—and with that they both survived and grew.

By the time fall came, the bird could fly again. It flew uncertainly at first. But as winter approached and cold set in, Rosa felt the bird should fly south. One day she took it to the open window and held it up so it could fly away.

You wouldn't have done that? No, perhaps I wouldn't have either. It was hard for Rosa to do it. But she loved the little bird so much that she thought more of its happiness than of her own. We don't often love anything that much.

"You are free, little bird," she whispered to it. "You're free and winter is coming. Fly away to the south where it's warm and the fields and woods are full of good things to eat."

But the bird, to her surprise and intense delight, did not fly away to the south. It flew up to her shoulder, gave a little chirp, and perched there quietly.

Now a very great event was being celebrated in Italy that winter.

This was—remember—a long time ago, almost at the beginning of everything. And it happens that that year was the first year people ever celebrated Christmas.

I don't mean (said St. Francis) that it was the year Jesus was born. The birth of Jesus was hardly a celebration. Mary and Joseph, two weary travelers, came late one night to a little town named Bethlehem where they couldn't even find a room in the inn and had to find lodging in a stable. There Jesus was born. But you know that. I've shown you what the event was like by this crèche I've built. A few shepherds came, some angels flew down singing, and on Twelfth Night the Three Kings brought their gifts. After that, nobody remembered the birthday for hundreds of years.

But at last, hundreds of years after Jesus was born, the emperor of Rome became a Christian. When he did, he decided one day that they should have a special holiday to celebrate the birthday of Jesus.

So he consulted the church fathers. At first they didn't know what

day His birthday fell on, but they decided it should be—what day? Right. The twenty-fifth day of December.

When the people heard Christmas was to be celebrated, they rejoiced. Don't you? Is there anything you love more than a holiday? And is any holiday as wonderful as Christmas?

Different people had different thoughts about ways to celebrate it. But about one thing everyone agreed.

This was a birthday. There is only one way to celebrate a birthday! That is to give the one who has the birthday a gift. Throughout all the world people began thinking about what gift they might give the Holy Infant—for had there ever been such another birthday as His?

When the great day came, everyone poured out of their houses to go to church. You never saw such a merry crowd—or such a quantity of lace and ribbon! Everyone who went to church wanted to look more magnificent than anyone else who was there.

And everyone wanted everyone else to see how generously he gave. You never saw such gifts. It is impossible to list all the things—gold and silver and jewels and houses and lands and cattle and grain and paintings and statues and even churches. There had never been such a gala occasion in the history of giving as that first Christmas. Everyone in the world must have put on his finest attire and gone to church to give his Christmas gift.

Everyone except Rosa.

She had been going to church every day for months. Every day, from the moment she had heard there was to be a Christmas, she had prayed before the statue she loved best. This was the statue of the Virgin with her Baby in her arms. She had prayed that she might have a gift to give. For she had nothing—not a single coin, not a single thing she could sell to gain a coin, not so much as a ribbon. Nothing.

Every day for months on her way home from the church she had looked about her eagerly, hoping for some miracle like maybe finding a penny. But she found nothing. A month before Christmas it snowed. After that, since she had no shoes, she had to run to and from the church to keep her bare feet from freezing. She could take no time to loiter and look; besides, the snow covered everything.

So on Christmas Day she did not go to church when all the others did. She sat alone—and prayed, I hope—unless she had gotten too miserable to pray! I know she cried. The tears ran down her face in burning streams.

She was so miserable she didn't even think to eat, which was just as well, because I don't believe she had anything to eat.

Perhaps this is why the bird began to chirp. He got hungry. It was a weak chirp because that was all the sound he ever made, but it caused Rosa to look at him.

If you were only a fat goose, she thought, or even a plump young pigeon, I could give you. But he was not. He was just a plain little bird, not much bigger than a sparrow.

Still he was something. In fact, he was all she had. Why should she not give him to the Christ Child? But could she? The Child, she felt, would accept him. But the priests, she was sure, would turn her and her bird away. And the people—how they would laugh to see her bringing such a sparrow as a birthday gift to Him who was the King of Heaven!

But perhaps if she waited till it was dark—darkness comes early on Christmas Day—she could steal into the church unseen and leave her gift without anyone noticing who she was or what she had brought.

As night came down, Rosa slipped out into the street, which was almost empty by then. Clutching the little cage of twigs tightly to her, she ran swiftly to the church, darted up the steps, and in a moment had slipped inside.

It was dark inside, though here and there a candle burned. But Rosa knew the church by heart and quickly found her way through the shadowed emptiness to the statue of the Virgin with the Baby Jesus in her arms.

You wonder why she didn't leave her little bird at the crèche? I'm sure that's where you would have left him, and so would I. So would Rosa, had there been a crèche. But this is the thirteenth century, and that was almost a thousand years ago. There were no crèches in those days. Can you believe this crèche I've built is the first one there ever has been? But that's the way it is with everything. Everything has to start somewhere.

So since Rosa had no creche, she took her gift to the best place she knew to take it, the Virgin and her Baby.

A few votive candles still burned before the statue. Rosa had never lit a candle since she had no money to give, but she had lit many in her mind.

What's that you say? You think you get more light from wax ones. I think you'll find that's questionable.

But as I was saying, Rosa knelt before the statue of the Virgin and prayed. I don't know how long she prayed. Like everyone who prays a lot, Rosa, I'm sure, had found prayer has nothing to do with time. A great deal of time can pass and nothing important happens. And in no time at all a miracle can occur.

Suddenly something strange began to occur. Rosa didn't speak a word aloud, nor did she hear an actual voice. Yet suddenly a conversation began between Rosa and the Lord.

"What are you doing here, Rosa?" said the Lord.

Was it the Baby Jesus who spoke? I can't say because the voice was not a voice Rosa heard with her ears. This conversation took place in—I suppose I would have to say—the mind, like the candles she lit.

But the voice was no less real because she heard it in her mind, since that's the only place you hear voices anyway. It startled Rosa. She looked about to see if someone was there she hadn't seen.

Then she heard herself saying, "I've come to bring my gift on Your birthday."

"You are late," said the Lord. "My birthday is almost over and I wondered if you were coming. I hoped you would."

"Thank You, Lord," said Rosa. "I just thought I'd wait till the people had gone home and the church was empty."

"Don't you like my worshipers?" said the Lord. "Or do you think they might not like you?"

Rosa said nothing.

"What is that you have in your hands?" said the Lord softly at last.

"My gift," said Rosa.

"And what is that?" said the Lord.

Rosa did not know what to say. She couldn't bring herself to tell the Lord that all she had for Him on His birthday was a little sparrow in a cage of twigs. At last she said, "I have brought you all I had to give."

This time it was the Lord who for a long time had nothing to say. I am sure He was looking at the little girl very closely, and taking everything in—the bare feet, the thin shift, the thin arms and legs, the pale face, the huge hungry eyes. Do you suppose, as He looked, a tear or two stole down His face? The Bible says that once He wept. I don't mean tears of sorrow, but tears of love.

"That is a very great gift," He said at last. "Not even the emperor has given me that. What is it you are giving me?"

Silently Rosa held out the little cage of twigs.

"When you give all you have to give," said the Lord, "you almost always find you have more to give than you dreamed. Let me see what you have."

Shyly Rosa opened the door of the cage and took out the little bird. He huddled for a moment in her hands, and as always she could feel his heart beating wildly. Then as if he, too, knew what to do he flew up and hovered on whirring wings just above the face of the Infant, and it seemed to Rosa that as he hovered there, he stretched forward and his beak touched the mouth of the Infant as if in a kiss.

Then he flew away into the darkness of the church.

The girl gave a little cry of alarm to see the bird disappear. Then she heard the Lord again. "You are the gift love has given to life," He was saying. "Go, O Love of Life, and give to life what you have to give."

And at that moment out of the dark came such a shower of notes as Rosa had never heard.

The nightingale had found its song!

Rosa's bird that had had no song was suddenly singing, and it was singing as no bird before had ever sung, for Rosa's bird was the nightingale. If you have never stood alone in the dark and heard a nightingale's song, I doubt if I can tell you what it is like. Poets have tried, but how imperfectly!

It was not just a song. It was a flood, a tumult, an exuberant excess, joy rejoicing in its joyousness, passion pouring forth in prodigal invention, life delighting in aliveness, giving unstintedly, without holding back. It was the song of one who gives all he has to give, only to find he has yet more and more.

Then as suddenly as it had begun the singing stopped. Rosa stared up into the darkness. She sensed that her bird was gone. But the song was not gone. It sang on in her. And the nightingale has been singing on for us ever since.

What's that you want to know? What happened to Rosa? After that, what could happen to her? I've heard she lived a long, full, happy life. But she'd already done that, hadn't she? Hadn't she? She'd given all she had to give and found that her gift was a nightingale's song that men have thrilled to hear for a thousand years. You can't do more than that, can you? Not even if like Methuselah you live to be more than nine hundred!

What's that you say? Maybe it all happened in Rosa's imagination?

Maybe it did. Can you think of any great and wonderful thing that doesn't happen there? Mainly, at least.

Take this creche I've built. Where did it happen if not in imagination? Or a church. Or a story. Or the nightingale's song—certainly a song!

And one thing to think about, until Rosa and the Lord's power touched him, the nightingale was just a plain little bird. After that he was the nightingale.

What's that? Nightingales don't sing in winter, they sing in spring? So they do. And aren't we lucky to have them then!

But this nightingale, the first nightingale, Rosa's bird—as I have just told you—sang that Christmas, the first Christmas we ever celebrated. Yes, that is where the nightingale learned to sing.

Maybe it wasn't this way at all—is that what you are thinking? Maybe Rosa's bird had always been able to sing, always been a nightingale? But he had been hurt. Then, there in the church, flying free in the dark, he began to sing again? Very well. If that's what you want to believe. Some people explain away every miracle.

Yet I have heard that sometimes—if you go alone, as Rosa went, and as I too have gone—not on Christmas Eve when the church is full of people, but late on Christmas night—or for that matter any time when there is nobody there but you and the Lord—I've heard that some (not all, but some!) have sometimes heard such music as poured from Rosa's bird. Or do you think perhaps it was an angel I heard singing?

Are You Sure It's Snowing Beyond the Next Corner?

"IT WAS THE kind of happening you're reluctant to talk about," Madison said.

The party had ended hours ago, but three of us still lingered beside the fire. From time to time one of us got up and poked at it or went out onto the porch and brought in a log to throw on it.

The only light besides the fire was from the lights on the Christmas tree at the other end of the room; it was Christmas Eve.

It was inevitable that we should get to talking about Christmases past; the three of us had shared so many. I started it with a tale about a Christmas I had spent in a cabin in the Rockies, with snow piled twelve feet deep outside the door.

Then Joe Whitmarsh told about what he said was "the loneliest Christmas of my life—and not because I was alone." It was a small boy's story about a broken home and a drunken stepfather and no Christmas at all—no tree, no gifts, no anything except a boy's fear of what life might hold in store for him.

We sat for a long time after he had finished, silently watching the flames pulse in the glowing logs until suddenly one of the logs burst open and a plume of golden sparks erupted from its heart.

That is when Madison began, "It was the kind of happening you're reluctant to talk about." He stopped and sat silent for such a long time I thought he was not going to talk about it. Then he went on: "Or perhaps, after a long time, if you do talk about it, you tell it to a friend or two you feel know you very well—well enough to know you're not a madman.

"Both of you have known me many years. I'm a matter-of-fact sort, wouldn't you say? Certainly I'm not given to superstition or self-deception, am I?"

Whitmarsh and I shook our heads.

"This happened a long time ago. On Christmas Eve. No doubt that's why I'm telling it now. And that may have prepared my mind for it to happen.

"Christmas is a time when emotion has sway over most of us. It brings all kinds of feelings to the surface of the mind. Feelings that ordinarily lie securely locked away from thought—expectations, hopes, fears, old memories of events and people—more like ghosts than like realities. They bubble up and send thought swirling in unforeseen directions.

"I'll admit my mind's often in a state of excitement at Christmastime. But that in no way explains the event I'm going to tell you'':

* * * * *

Looking back, I sometimes wonder—did it really happen? Though when it happened it was the realest experience I ever had. That's the way it always is when it happens to you. But when such an event didn't happen to you—you just hear someone tell you about it—you always wonder if he's inclined to drink or to fantasy. And you may be right to wonder. Perhaps such an event can't happen when reason's firmly in the saddle. Something has to make us open to more than what's reasonable.

With me, that something was Christmas Eve. I was in a strange city. I'd been away from home for a week on a business trip. I was feeling very lonely and altogether sorry for myself. I was engaged to be married to the loveliest girl on earth—so you can see how many years ago this was, I married her thirty-eight years ago—and here I was spending Christmas Eve sitting in a hotel room all by myself instead of spending Christmas Eve with her. I wanted to be with Sylvia. I wanted to see her, to hear her voice, to hold her in my arms, to tell her I loved her. I wanted it more than anything on earth. Even now, when I think of Sylvia, I think I know how a drug addict must feel.

So I sat in my room cursing everything that separates lovers. I cursed the dismal world I found myself in, the ugly city I found myself in, the barny hotel I found myself in, the bare room I found myself in, the uncomfortable chair I found myself in, and the even more uncomfortable bed I found myself in when I threw myself down on that. I cursed all business in general and especially the business I was in, that had taken me away from the girl I loved. As I lay in the bed I vowed I'd make so much money no one—nothing—would ever be able to separate Sylvia and me on a Christmas Eve again.

But I'm not the kind that stays miserable long, so having felt sorry for myself as long as I was able, I put on my overcoat and went out. A bellboy had told me of a famous restaurant only a few blocks away. I decided to try it.

There was a huge menu and I read it clear through—I had nothing else to do. It informed me, among other matters, that this restaurant had been there since early Colonial days. Perhaps even that helped set the stage for the events I'm about to relate.

The restaurant was gay with Christmas decorations. A violinist moved among the tables, playing romantic numbers and Christmas carols. The food was as excellent as the bellboy at the hotel had assured me it would be. The waiter showed no disposition to hurry me, in fact he was inclined to conversation; I'm sure he sensed how lonely and in need of cheering up I was.

As the only other thing I had to do was to go back to my hotel room, I spent a very leisurely time at the table. I listened to the music, I watched the people at the other tables, I talked to the waiter, I wandered among my own reveries, I ate heartily, and it is possible I drank heartily, too—at least for me.

But at last, glancing about, I noticed almost all the other tables were empty. I looked at my watch—the hands were moving toward midnight. I hurriedly paid my bill and left.

When I came out into the street, there was no taxi at the door. But it was a lovely, star-filled night, and the air, though it was brisk, wasn't uncomfortable. As my hotel was close, I decided to walk back to it.

I don't know how I did it—I'm usually a person who has a keen sense of direction—but somehow when I started from the restaurant, I must have turned left when I should have turned right. For I found myself plunging down narrow streets that led me not back toward my hotel, but to the river. However, the night was pleasant. The river—I knew—was only a few blocks out of my way. So I decided to walk along the river's edge before I made my way back. I even thought a taxi might happen along—if it did I would hail it.

How long I walked I don't know. I'll have to admit my mind was more on Sylvia than on getting back to that hotel. But at last I realized it was time to turn back. I was sure I knew in what direction the hotel lay, so I left the river and struck out up a side street. It was a poorly lighted street—I remember thinking that. The farther I walked, the poorer and darker and narrower the street became. I felt I was moving through an area of dilapidated and mostly empty warehouses, all very old and very poor.

At every corner I looked for street signs, but there seemed to be none. Finally I decided this street couldn't possibly be leading me back toward the heart of the city.

So at the next corner I turned left again.

But if the street I'd been on seemed dark and narrow, this street was darker and narrower yet. It was scarcely more than an alleyway.

But unlike the street I'd been on, this was a residential street. The residences were row houses, but I had a feeling the houses were unusually substantial and extremely well-kept. You come on such neighborhoods in big cities—unmapped oases.

This was only a feeling, however. For as I started down the street, I realized it was snowing. Yes, snowing hard. It took me completely by surprise. I'd been so preoccupied with finding my way, I hadn't paid the least attention to the fact the weather was changing. I was in the midst of a heavy snowstorm. The snow was coming down so thick and fast I could hardly see where I was. The street was so narrow and the snow so thick, it was like walking through a tunnel. I almost had to feel my way along. What was more—impossible as this had to be—the snow seemed so deep underfoot it was hard slogging through it.

Yet though now I was concerned about the snow, I was no longer concerned about my direction. I knew exactly where I was going.

I was going to a house. Yes, a house on this very street. For I stopped before a house, mounted a low flight of steps, and pounded at the door till a man opened it.

"Merry Christmas!" I said.

"Merry Christmas!" said the man, grasping my hand. "Thank heaven you're here. We began to wonder if you'd make it."

"So did I," I said.

The man peered out at the street before he shut the door behind me. "Isn't this some snow? It's been coming down like this since afternoon. But it's a white Christmas."

Now I'd like to make things clear. Looking back, I've no idea who this man was. I don't remember ever having seen him in my life. Yet when I shook his hand there in that hall, I knew him—knew him as well as I know either of you, and you're the best friends I have.

Strangely, too, I knew this man's name. I knew the names of everyone I met that night, knew them as well as I know yours, and I called all these people by name. But I can't remember a single name, no, not of any of them.

As you know, my name is Austin, Austin Madison. That man called me by my name. So did the others who were there. But the name they called me was neither Austin nor Madison. I've tried—oh, I've tried—but I can't remember what name they gave me. Except I know it wasn't Austin. But I responded to it—whatever name it was—as if it were my own. It *was* my own.

I stood in the hall of that strange house I knew as well as I know this one—with a strange man I knew as well as I know you—knocking a thick snow that had been falling since afternoon (though I'd have sworn it hadn't been falling five minutes earlier) from my boots—though I'd walked out of my hotel that evening in a pair of plain brown shoes I'd purchased two weeks earlier in Kansas City. But it was boots I had on, as did he.

In fact, all my clothes were much like his. I don't remember exactly what they were, but I was dressed stylishly—stylishly, that is, for two hundred years ago. Yes, two hundred years ago. I've looked at lots of pictures.

The man put his arm around me and the two of us went into the next room. The room was filled with people.

"Look who just came in out of the snow!" said the man. Everyone let out a shout of welcome. Several men came up and shook my hand. I went about greeting the women. It was obvious this was a Christmas party, not too unlike the one here tonight. There were punch and food, and I took a little of both.

During the next few minutes I talked about various things with a number of those people. What did we talk about? I can't recall except in the vaguest way.

I can see you wonder how this can be. As incredible as this experience was, you'd think surely every detail of it was deeply etched into my mind.

I've wondered about it as much as you. The house, the furniture, the clothes we had on, the people's names, the conversation—why isn't it all, every bit of it, still with me vividly?

I see you shake your heads. Don't think I haven't shaken mine, I've wrung it! For years I couldn't understand it. Until finally it came to me: It's because there was nothing strange or unusual about it—the house, the conversation, all that.

The moment I stepped into that hall and that man came forward to meet me, I was no longer Austin Madison, observing a strange scene. I was the man in boots and cape with the name he had given me. This was a house I was familiar with. I was with a man I knew. I paid no more attention to my clothes or to my surroundings or to what we were saying than I did here tonight. The room was filled with chatter, and I entered into it—the usual conversations you have when you walk into a room filled with friends. And it didn't enter my head there was

was Sylvia. Yes, my wife. The woman I married thirty-eight years ago.

And this is perhaps the strangest part of this strange affair. Sylvia, the woman who walked into the room, didn't look like Sylvia. No, not at all. As all of you know, Sylvia was a blonde. This woman was a brunette. My wife was of a fair size, this woman was small. This woman had a slender face, my wife's was round. Her feet were tiny, much smaller than Sylvia's. I remember her feet, because her feet were all I could see—she had on a long skirt, as did all the women in the room. But in spite of all these differences of appearance, there was no question. Sylvia had just walked into the room. As she paused in the doorway, our eyes met.

Do you know what it is to look into the eyes of someone you love and have someone you love look at you? It's not something that has to do with eyes. It's something between souls. At least *soul* seems the best word for it.

If she looked at me, I'd know Sylvia anywhere I ever saw her. And it would make no difference what her appearance was. She could have on a disguise. A magician could change her into something strange. I'd know her. Something would pass between us. I know, for it always has. Something particularly ours—and there's no mistaking it. One look out of her eyes, that's all I would need. And that's all I needed there.

Sylvia walked into that room and looked at me, and all the other people in it vanished. Oh, I don't mean physically, but from my mind. Lovers are alone even in a crowded room—have you ever noticed that?

Love is a curious closeness. It has nothing to do with distance—or time either, I guess.

Sometimes when I'm traveling and go into a motel room at night, I have the strongest feeling that if I just knew how to look, I'd see her right there with me. Yes, I still do. Haven't you ever felt like that? You can't measure it with a yardstick—or a timepiece either.

More rapidly than politeness probably permitted, I was across the room and had her hand in mine.

As I've said, there's much about this experience I don't remember clearly. But the look in her eyes, the touch of her fingertips—those are still as vivid in my mind as that fire there!

When lovers touch, what is it? Something electric, wouldn't you say? A kind of carbon-arc effect, it writhes across your skin and through your veins and down into the marrow of your bones, and you tingle! Even now as I talk about it, my fingers shake with the unforgettable intensity—yes, across two hundred years.

You'd have thought we'd have something great to say to one another at such a moment. But we didn't.

"Merry Christmas!" I said, and she said, "Merry Christmas!"

But then, what else could we say on Christmas Eve in a room full of people?

And if all the great and famous lovers who have ever written love poems had uttered all their most beautiful phrases of deathless passion and ardent affection in one mighty chorus, all their utterances together wouldn't have stirred in me deeper depths of love! I was with the woman I loved, we looked into one another's eyes, we touched one another's hands, we heard one another's voices.

I don't know how I got her out of that room, but of course I did. In a few minutes I was holding her in my arms and saying to her over and over, "I love you, I love you, I love you," and she was saying to me, "I love you."

After that we said nothing. There's a private country of the heart only lovers know the way to. And the language spoken there doesn't depend on words. That's where we went and that's the language we spoke. I hope you've been there. I can't tell you what it's like.

How long a time passed it's hard to say—five minutes or a hundred years. Maybe there's no difference—I often wonder now. And I'm sure I couldn't have told you then—when you're with the girl you love, you don't pay much attention to the time.

I'd come there to be with the girl I loved—we were to be married in March—that's all I'd come for. Or almost all.

I'd come to tell her something. Something terribly important. Something I didn't know how to tell her. But I had to. I had to tell her I was going to leave. Leave that very night. I hoped she would understand. But I knew she wouldn't like it. I didn't like it either. Oh, I was excited about it, but full of dread, too. But I had to go, and I'd come to tell her this. I took a long time getting around to it.

"They've been fighting for six months up north now," I said at last.

She was a long time speaking. "I've heard."

"We've got an army up in Canada. I ought to be up there with them."

"No, this is where you ought to be. Here. With me. Always." She drew me tight against her.

"I've got to go," I said. "I've got to. My friends are waiting for me now. At the inn. I've promised to go with them. They're leaving at dawn. I'm going with them."

"No," she said. "Oh, no. Don't go. Please don't go."

"I must," I said. "In a time like this, a man hasn't any choice."

"I thought I was your choice?"

"You are. You know that. But I promised them I'd go with them. They'll be waiting."

"And won't I be waiting? You'll not be back."

"Oh, but I will. I'll be here for our wedding. You can count on that."

"No," she said again. "Don't go. Don't go. You won't come back."

"I will. All eternity couldn't keep me from making you my wife. I promise you that."

I've often wondered. Except for those few hours we had together that night, I don't know what happened back there. But I don't think I made that wedding date in March. I think I kept that promise just thirty-eight years ago.

(Again Madison stopped and sat silent for a long time. So long that I thought I ought to say something, though I knew if Whitmarsh or I broke the current of his thought we probably would hear no more. For I could see that it was only with great effort that he spoke.)

I had brought a gift—two golden lockets.

"One is for you and one is for me," I said. "For Christmas. Open them."

She took them in her hand and opened them. There was a portrait in each. I'd had them painted—one of her, one of me.

"Oh, they're beautiful," she said.

"I'll wear one, you'll wear the other," I said. "We'll wear each other next to our hearts."

"I already do that," she said.

I fastened the chain around her neck. "Do you think this chain will hold you till I get back?"

"You don't need any chains," she said. "I'm yours as long—as long as you want me."

"Then you're mine forever," I said.

"Forever and ever," she said.

What more is there to tell? Two young people loving one another. Hours passed, I suppose. All I know is, it was almost morning when I left. As I'd told her, I'd promised to go back to the inn by dawn. And I had to keep that promise.

She came with me to the door. "Good-bye," I said. "No, not good-bye. *Au revoir.* I'll be back before you even miss me."

"I'll miss you when you walk out that door," she said. "I'm missing you already—at the thought of your going." She began to cry softly. "You're the only man I've ever wanted, the only man I'll ever want. Remember that always."

"Don't cry," I said, kissing her eyes. "I love you."

She reached up and pulled my mouth down to hers. "Don't leave me, please," she said. "I love you."

I held her as tightly as I could. Then I turned away and ran down the steps. I had to run. It was the only way I could go.

I looked back once through the snow. She was standing in the doorway. Then the snow blotted everything out. It was still coming down hard.

I walked down the tunnel of a street, alone in the utter pitch-black darkness and the silent falling snow that blotted out the world of space and time.

Then suddenly I was back in space and time again. I took a step and my foot fell on bare sidewalk.

I looked down. My feet were shod not in boots, but in the plain brown shoes I'd bought in Kansas City. They were not plodding through the snow. There was no snow, no snow at all. The pavement was dry. I looked up. The stars were shining. I lifted my hands before my face. My wristwatch glittered on my wrist—I remember, it was exactly ten minutes after six. I looked at my clothes. They were my everyday ordinary clothes. I stood there for a moment and stared around me.

I was Austin Madison. I was in the twentieth century. I was on an ordinary street in a familiar city. And at that moment a taxicab roared up beside me. I held out my hand, it stopped, and in five minutes I was back at my hotel. When I woke—it was the middle of the next afternoon—I found I had never gone to bed; I'd just thrown myself down into a chair and slept there.

I was hardly awake before I was back looking for that street and house. You can guess that. I looked till it was dark, up and down street after street. The next day I looked again. I asked people all kinds of crazy questions. And they looked at me as if I were crazy.

I found nothing. The next day I had to take a train home.

When I got home, the first thing I did was change our plans. Sylvia and I hadn't intended to get married till March—March again, strange, isn't it?—but I wasn't going to take a chance this time. Three days after I got home, we got married. That was thirty-eight years ago.

As you know, my wife died two years ago. Yes, it was almost this time of year. A week after she passed, I went back to that city. I had a business reason but that was only an excuse.

I suppose I was hoping against hope I might find—but what?

I wandered about the older section of the city for several days. Then the day before Christmas, in a small shop down by the river I found—this.

* * * * *

Madison held out his hand. It was shaking. In it was a golden locket.

"One of the lockets?" I asked.

"Yes, the one I kept for myself. With her picture in it." He offered it to me. "Open it."

I took it from his hand and pressed the clasp. It opened. In it was a portrait. I gazed at it for a moment. Then I looked up at him with a smile.

"What a lovely idea," I said. "To have a portrait of Sylvia painted to put in this. It's a beautiful likeness." I handed it to Whitmarsh. He walked to the fire and studied it by firelight.

"A perfect likeness!" he said. "Beautiful!"

"Did you have it painted from a photograph?" I said.

Madison looked at us strangely. He took the locket back, holding it still open in his hand, looking from it to us and back again. "Let me understand," he said. "You see here a portrait of Sylvia, my wife, the woman you knew?"

"Of course," I said. "It's perfect."

"A beautiful miniature!" said Whitmarsh. "The artist did a perfect job."

"But there was no artist," said Madison. "I have no portrait of Sylvia."

Now it was my turn to look at Madison strangely.

"But—" I said, "that is a portrait of Sylvia."

Madison said nothing.

"Isn't it?" I said. I pointed to the locket in his hand. "Isn't that what you see there?"

Still he said nothing.

"What do you see?" I said slowly.

"I see—" said Madison, and stopped. He looked at me. He looked at Whitmarsh. He looked at the locket. At that moment the dying fire leaped up and cast a glow upon his face. I don't know what he was looking at. I wish I did. For as I looked into his eyes, I knew what it is like when you look with eyes of love.

He closed the locket tenderly. "I see," he said, "the woman I love." Then he cleared his throat and looked at his watch. "It's almost morning. We should have been in bed hours ago."

I walked to the window, pulled back the curtain, and glanced out. "It's been snowing. It's a white Christmas!"

Madison laughed. "Are you sure it's snowing beyond the next corner? That may be a couple of hundred years away."

Conversation at an Inn

"YOU! A CAPTAIN in the Roman army! I can't believe it, Philip!" said Adam. "And you, Balsha? A merchant in—where did you say?"

"Nisibis."

"Nisibis! I hardly know where it is," said Adam. "Up near Assyria, isn't it? Almost the end of the earth."

"Hardly that," said Balsha. "The earth, I've discovered, is a big place, Adam."

Adam shook his head, looking from one of his friends to the other. "I envy you two. You've been everywhere, and here I still am where I've always been, in the inn of my father and his father before him."

"And are we glad you are!" said Philip. "The way this town's packed by this census, thank Jupiter I know the innkeeper!"

"Thank Jupiter?" said Adam. "The Roman army hasn't made a pagan out of you, has it?"

Philip scratched the back of his head. "After twenty years in the Roman army, I'm not sure what I am. I guess I don't think it's important what I call myself—or God."

Adam turned to Balsha. "You, Balsha? You haven't abandoned the faith, have you?"

"Oh, I think I'm still a Jew," said Balsha, "though like Philip, I've been a lot of places and met a lot of people this last twenty years. You get a few new ideas. You'd expect that, wouldn't you?"

"That all depends on what the ideas are," said Adam.

"I'm from Nisibis. You said it's the end of the world. But out beyond, there's a whole other world. I've journeyed there. You know about Persia, of course."

Adam nodded.

"And India?"

Adam nodded, a little more slowly.

"And China?"

Adam shook his head.

"I've heard of it," said Philip.

"The people of China have yellow skin and a civilization so old they think they're the only civilized people in the world—all the rest of us are barbarians—so they've built a wall a thousand miles long and so big the Roman army could march on it, around their entire kingdom, just to keep us out. I've been there. China. India. Persia. Strange lands. Different people. New ideas. Adam, you ask me if I'm a Jew. I don't know. You're a Roman citizen now, aren't you, Philip?"

Philip nodded.

"I figured you'd be. Me? I'm a citizen of the world. I've found out there are fascinating people everywhere. Their cities, their customs, their ideas. Yes, and their religions! Why do you think I'm a merchant? Just to make money? No. Because it pushes me out past my old horizons. How is it the poet puts it? I make the golden journey to Samarkand! And beyond. Beyond. I'm searching, Adam. Searching."

"What are you searching for?" said Adam.

"What are we all searching for?" said Philip. "For the truth. Aren't you?"

"You think you're going to find the truth by traveling over the earth?" said Adam.

"That's surely one of the places we have to look, isn't it?" said Philip. "Where would you look?"

"Is there any doubt?" said Adam. "I'd look in the Bible, the Torah, the word of God."

"I look there, too," said Balsha. "But as to just what that truth means, different people have different ideas, even the rabbis—don't they? Yes, I'm searching for the truth. That's why I'm here. Oh, I'm here because the Roman Emperor ordered a census and I was born in this town. But that's only one of the reasons I'm here. I live in Nisibis. Nisibis may belong to Rome, but it isn't Roman. It's a Persian town. Some of my best friends are Persian priests. They're called magi. Ever heard of them?"

His friends nodded.

"They're very wise men. Just as much monotheists as we Jews. And these magi have a teaching. Have you two ever heard of the Messiah?"

"I'm in the Roman army, I've heard of everything," said Philip.

"I've heard of it, that's all," said Adam.

"The magi believe that from time to time a child is to be born who is the Son of God. The Persians call him Shaoshyant, but I believe the Hebrew word is Messiah."

"Shaoshyant or Messiah, I don't believe in him," said Adam, shaking his head.

"There are Jews who do," said Balsha.

"In Nisibis perhaps. Not here. God is to have a son?" Adam threw up his hands in a gesture of disbelief.

earth has. Even the ancient Greeks thought that. Plato wished to go and study with them."

"The Greeks have as many crack-brain notions as the Romans," said Philip. "Or the Persians!"

Balsha flushed. Then he said in a deeply earnest voice, "The magi are wise men! Great astronomers and astrologers, and they've prophesied this for a thousand years. Now they say, all the signs—all the signs!—point to now. Right now! Please don't shut your minds to this. When he comes, I want to be there. Don't you?"

"I probably will be," said Philip. "In my official capacity. This Messiah—straighten me out if this isn't true, Balsha, but I think I've heard it—when he comes he's going to proclaim himself King of the Jews."

Balsha nodded.

"And he's supposed to rescue them from their oppressors, no?"

"He will, he will," said Balsha.

"That means Rome, doesn't it?" said Philip.

"I'll second that," said Adam. "If the shoe fits—or should I say iron boot?"

"This is no joke," said Philip. "If there's one thing any Messiah had better keep in mind, the Roman army takes a dim view of people who proclaim themselves kings. There's only one power that decides who's going to be king of anything, that's Caesar. We've already got one king of the Jews."

"Herod!" said Adam and spat.

"I have the same opinion of him you do," said Philip. "All the more reason why we don't need two. We've got enough problems without Messiahs stirring up trouble."

"Stirring up trouble!" cried Balsha. "You can't believe that. You know in your heart the son of God could only bring—what is it the Bible says?—righteousness in His wings, and order and liberty and love. He'll be the prince of peace."

"You really believe all this, don't you?" said Philip.

"Yes, I do."

"And you've searched for this son of God, this Messiah, whatever he's called?"

"I have."

"Is that why you went to India?"

"Yes, and the people there—they're very spiritual, the most

spiritual people I've ever met—they have the same beliefs the magi have."

"That God takes human form?"

"Yes."

"And you found Him there?"

"You know I didn't," said Balsha.

"No, of course, you didn't. And this China, you went there, too, you said?"

Balsha nodded. "It's an unbelievable country, across the roof of the world. The mountains there make Ararat and Olympus look like foothills. And among those mountains there are men as spiritually lofty as the mountains. They spend their whole lives in prayer and meditation, holy, holy men. And do you know what they believe? God appears as a human child."

"And among these you found your human god? No, you didn't," said Philip, not waiting for an answer. "But now you expect to find Him here. In Palestine! Why?"

"Don't you see?" said Balsha excitedly. "I don't know why it didn't occur to me long ago, and I a Jew! If God is going to have a son, where better than here? Has any people been more His than we Jews? The magi agree. Some of them are in Jerusalem now."

"He's to be born in Jerusalem?" said Philip.

"I—I think so," said Balsha.

"You're not sure?"

Balsha shook his head.

"Anyway, you haven't found Him yet?"

"Not yet," said Balsha.

"Not ever, Balsha, never! I've met lots of holy men. Probably as many as you. Remember, the Roman army gets around. Yes, and holy women—along with quite a few unholy ones." He laughed. "Saviors are always popping up. You know what I've found them to be? Sometimes rogues. Yes, charming and persuasive rogues. But most of them weren't rogues. They were the projection of the delusion of their own followers, and as much under the delusion as their followers were; they believed they were divine. But that didn't make them so. No matter how many millions of worshipers knelt at their feet. When someone like me came along—not hypnotized by his will-to-believe—it was clear, the human god was merely human. If there's anything I've learned as a Roman soldier, it's that there are no saviors. I've encountered a lot of strange gods and goddesses and sons and daughters of gods in my life, but I've never met any of them when the chips were down, who could do me much good—or was much help in a sword fight."

"You don't sound as if you even believe in God any more," said Adam.

"That all depends on what you mean by God. Personally I think I believe more in a real, honest-to-god God than either you or Balsha."

"God is God," said Adam.

"Words are words," said Philip. "I probably don't believe in the kind of God you do, and I'm sure I don't believe in the kind Balsha says he believes in. I don't believe there's somebody out there"—he pointed at the sky—"some kind of super Caesar on a starry throne who will maybe help me if I ask him to—or maybe won't. All this Savior stuff—help me, Almighty King—come and deliver us, Lord, from our own foolishness—it's a lot of superstition.

"The kind of God I believe in is a force within myself. The God, the only real God, is the Spirit within me. You want to find your Lord and Savior? That's where you have to look for Him. Not in some far-off heaven or some Shaoshyant or Messiah. Look within yourself.

"Yes, I believe in God. I believe He made me in His image, just like I read it in the Torah as a boy. I believe He put Himself in me and in every atom of His universe, and He said, 'Now it's up to you. You have in you all the qualities of heart and mind you need to save yourself and your world.' "

Adam snorted. "If this is true, we've been a little slow doing it, haven't we?"

"You can't blame God for that," said Philip. "He gave us all we need. But He made us like Himself. That means free! Balsha, you think God has a son. I do, too. I think you're His son. And you too, Adam. Me, too. All of us are. We all have God in us. We have a divine nature. But it's up to us to express it. When you use your own divine power and intelligence and love, then you're true to the only true God there is."

"Why, you don't believe in anything," said Adam. "You're a—a materialist."

"Materialist? No. I'm just not a superstitionist."

"No, Adam's right," said Balsha. "You don't believe in God. Your God—is He everything or nothing? At least, Adam and I believe in

God. Yes, the same God, the Lord God of the Torah."

"I believe in the Lord God of the Torah, but not in a God like yours, Balsha," said Adam quickly. "A God who becomes a human being? Never."

Philip laughed. "You have hit to the heart of the matter, Adam. A God who becomes like me? Heaven forbid! It's I who must become like God."

"You think you're like God?" said Adam. "You know what you sound like? You're just carrying the Roman heresy a step further. It's bad enough when they tell me I've got to worship Caesar as god—and they're trying to make us do that!—but you tell me I've got to worship you."

"That's ridiculous."

"Didn't you just say you're God?"

"I'm God. You're God. Every man is God."

"That's what I thought you said. Well, if man is God, it's not much of a God we have, is it?" said Adam.

"Yes, you call my belief superstition. I call yours blasphemy," said Balsha. "Here you sit, a Roman soldier in your iron suit, and you dare to tell me this is what God looks like? This is your idea of the divine? I'll stick to mine. A God of love. A God who loves us so much He sends His own begotten son to save us from our sins."

"You're not Jews," said Adam. "Neither of you. You're pagans. There is one supreme Lord of heaven and earth. He made me out of the clay, out of the dust. That's all you and I are, Philip. And all human beings. There is one God. I don't make images of Him—like me or anything else. I'm expressly forbidden to by His commandment. He is one, and there is none beside Him. No sons. No daughters. No uncles. No aunts.

"But enough of this. It's bedtime, and I've still got a job to do before I go to bed—or my wife won't let me in with her.

"You know with this census how crowded Bethlehem is. Well, three days ago, a couple came here looking for a room. Poor people, from the North, from Galilee."

"What's the old saying? Nothing good will come out of Galilee?" said Balsha.

Adam nodded. "This fellow comes up to my door. He's got his wife behind him, riding on a donkey. I wish I'd been the one to talk to him. But it was my wife. And you know women. It seems the man's wife is pregnant. Very pregnant. The child is due any minute. The woman's practically in labor as she rides up. And she's a mere wisp of a girl, hardly more than a child herself. My wife could see that.

"The inn is full, as you know. But my wife is too soft-hearted to turn them away. She can see they're poor people, simple people—he's a carpenter. They won't need fancy lodgings. So she tells them they can stay in the stable.

"So in the stable they've been staying. And just in time. That night the mother had her baby, a boy.

"Now, I'm under strict orders from my wife—she feels like she's the godmother—the last thing each night before I go to bed, I'm to make a trip to the stable and make sure everything's all right."

"Balsha, aren't you going with him?" said Philip.

"You want to go?" said Adam.

"Of course, he does," said Philip. "A newborn boy and just at the right time? He'll want to summon his magi."

"Philip, to me this is not a joke," said Balsha.

"I'm not joking. It's you. Are you going to be false to your own faith?"

"You know you don't think this actually might—"

"On the contrary. The whole point I've been making all night is—this *might*. Are you saying it mightn't?"

"You know how unlikely—"

"Your whole idea's unlikely. But don't you believe your own story?"

"Well, I don't," said Adam. "If this is the son of God, then God must be a carpenter."

"So He is," said Philip, "and an innkeeper and a merchant and a soldier in the Roman army."

"Look, that baby sleeping out there in my stable—and lucky to have a place to lay his head—is the son of a carpenter and a fourteen-year-old girl." Adam sounded irked. "But just so there can be no doubt, I think he was conceived out of wedlock. From something the mother let drop to my wife, we figure they've only been married a few months, not long enough to have a baby. That's your son of God for you."

"Adam, you're making it more interesting all the time," said Philip. "If he is a son of God, that last piece of information would make it more likely, wouldn't it, Balsha?"

Balsha looked as if he were not sure what he should say.

Adam snorted. "Let's be sensible. He's just a boy."

"You're belittling that? Neither of you has been hearing what I'm trying to tell you," said Philip. "Just a boy is all he needs to be to save the world. Yes, or even just a girl. Boy or girl, he has within him all he needs. He has God in him."

"If you insist on making a joke out of it, Philip, so will I," said Adam. "So I promise, if this boy, conceived out of wedlock, born in a stable, a simple carpenter's son, grows up and turns out to be a savior, I will write you a letter, Philip, swearing that I have been converted to your philosophy."

"Not to mine?" said Balsha.

"Oh, for heaven's sake, anything to get to bed! To yours, too! He's the son of God. You're the son of God. I'm the son of God. We're all the sons of God."

"I couldn't have said it better," said Philip. "And you, Balsha? He's the son of God?"

Balsha stammered for a moment. "Of course, I—I—"

"Are you two coming?" said Adam.

"Come on, Balsha," said Philip. "I promise you, you're going to see what a true son of God looks like."

"And I promise you, you're going to see a baby," said Adam.

"What else would one expect to see?" said Philip, as they started toward the door. "Have they named the baby yet?"

"Yes. Yes, they have. His name is—uh, let me think—Jesus."

The King of Heaven Is Coming Tonight

"THE KING OF HEAVEN is coming tonight!"

The news spread quickly over the valley. Even the scarecrow heard it, and no one hardly ever told him anything, because no one hardly ever spoke to him. But this was such important news that everyone was telling everyone.

The willow had heard it first. The wind told her. She told it to the first bird that lit in her branches. Once a bird heard it, he told everybody. Birds are even bigger gossips than the wind or the willows. They don't whisper, they put it in a song, and sing it out.

So in no time at all the news was everywhere. When the ox heard it, he ordered a meeting of all the creatures that lived in the valley. It would make too long a list to list all those who came, but they were all there—all, that is, unless you count those who do not listen to winds or willows or birds. There are, I am afraid, a large number of these; I hope you are not among them, for they miss many interesting happenings, as they did this night. Wholly unaware of the wonderful event that was about to occur, they drowsed by the fire in their homes. They probably even had the curtains drawn since it was late afternoon of a cold winter day when the news came.

But everybody else, from ox to mouse, including a couple of rabbits and a mole, and from the great gray goose to the littlest sparrow, including an owl that lived in the barn—they were all there.

"Are we all here?" said the ox, looking around sternly to see if someone might be missing. The ox took the lead in matters of importance. He had the biggest frame, so no one challenged him.

A chorus of "Yes, yes. We're all here," rose from the assembled beasts and birds, and the trees that formed a circle around them whispered gently, "Here, here."

"The scarecrow isn't here," said the mouse, pointing toward the shabby figure that stood silent and alone in the center of the farthest field.

"That!" screeched the guinea fowl. "That pile of sticks and straw and rags! Surely you don't count that as someone!"

"I just—I—" said the mouse.

"You're lucky we count you, mouse," said the guinea fowl with a sneer. "If you're going to count *him* as someone, what are you going to leave out?" The guinea fowl felt very important, and like many important fellows, he felt that for anybody to be someone, someone has to be nobody.

"I agree with the guinea fowl," said a starling. "Scarecrows don't even have a soul."

"We shouldn't say things like that about anything," said an oak tree. "Human beings don't believe you and I have a soul. I think souls aren't something we have, they're something we grow."

"We haven't come here to discuss theology," said the ox. "If we're all here except the scarecrow, we're all here. Now, willow, what is this news about the King of Heaven coming?"

"I had it from the wind," said the willow. "The King of Heaven is coming and He'll be here this very night. The wind said he passed Him down the road, hardly an hour or two away."

"The wind! Bah!" said an apple tree. "The wind's a rumor-monger."

"I won't hear that," said the oak. "The wind and I are friends. I'd trust the wind's tales before I trusted yours. Human beings once listened to you and that's the cause of all the trouble the world's been in ever since."

"Because they ate my fruit? I didn't ask them to," said the apple tree.

"And I don't know why they did," said a walnut tree, "your fruit is usually wormy."

This made the apple tree so angry it sulked down into its trunk and took no further part in the proceedings.

"Enough of this!" said the ox. "Now just what was it the wind told you?"

"What the wind said was this," said the willow: "Every year on this night, the King of Heaven makes a journey somewhere over the earth. Long ago when He was born, one of the mighty kings of the earth, jealous of His power and excellence, sent soldiers to kill Him. But the King of Heaven fled, seeking a place where He could hide and be safe."

"Sounds like a fable to me," said the goose. "Why didn't He just blast the soldiers with thunderbolts? I would have."

"That shows what a goose you are!" said a dove. "I have heard of this King. He is not a goose. Or a fable. He is kind and gentle. Like me."

"Go on with your story, willow," said the ox.

"All I know is what the wind told me," said the willow. "But I certainly think he knows more than a silly goose. And what he told me is this: Every year since then, on the anniversary of the night when He fled, the King of Heaven has returned to make a journey over the earth, looking for someone good and kind to give Him shelter."

At this all the creatures exclaimed, "If He's looking for someone good and kind, He's coming to the right place, isn't He?"

"To make sure of that," said the ox, "I shall, as is my custom, appoint committees to see that this place is a fitting shelter for a king."

So he appointed a committee for smoothing, and a committee for neatening, and a committee for straightening. Then he appointed a committee to greet the King. "Naturally I will head that," he said.

"The King will be hungry and thirsty," said the cow. "I will give Him a drink of my delicious milk."

"I will give Him one of my freshest eggs," said the chicken.

"I will dive into the pond and bring Him a fish," said the goose.

"I will let Him mount on my back and carry Him wherever He wishes to go," said the horse.

Everyone had something to give the King. Even the mole said he would mine the earth; he had no doubt he would strike gold.

The birds said they would fly in a vast flock overhead, executing such marvelous aerobatics the King would have to stand and cheer, though one of the swallows exclaimed: "I don't know that I will. Why does He have to come by night? Inconsiderate, that's what He is! We birds use the night for sleeping, which is what it's made for."

"Speak for yourself," said the owl. "I find night the ideal time to travel." At that a great argument arose. Most of the birds and most of the animals agreed with the swallow. But the rabbit and the mouse stood with the owl, though keeping a careful watch on her. So did a nighthawk that lived in the fencerow. The mole said, "Day and night, it's all one to me."

But the owl had the last word in the matter. "A king is a king," she said. "And He can be as inconsiderate as He wishes. It is not for us to question that. If He wishes to travel by night, night it must be."

By this time everyone was talking to everyone else about what they should and should not do, and they might still have been talking if suddenly the ox had not shouted: "We've work to do and lots of it. Get to work!"

At that everyone began scurrying and busying and bustling. But if anyone had been watching closely, I'm afraid what he might have seen was everyone mainly seeing to himself.

For naturally each one thought he would be the one the King would be especially looking at. So you never saw so much primping and prinking and preening and pruning, so much grooming and brushing and pluming. The trees dropped every dead leaf. The animals tugged out every burr and tangle from their coats. The birds fluffed themselves till not a feather was awry.

Only the scarecrow did nothing. No one asked him to do anything. Once a starling pointed to him and said: "That ragamuffin is a disgrace to the community! Isn't there something we can get him to do about himself?"

"He is a tatterdemalion, to be sure," said the ox. "But I think the best thing we can get him to do is nothing. Nothing is what he does best, isn't it?" At that everyone laughed.

But later the ox turned to the mouse. "You're his friend. Why don't you slip out there and ask him if he couldn't lie down where he won't be seen until the King is gone?"

"I don't know where you get the idea he's my friend," said the mouse. "He's not even one of my regular associates. But I'll see what I can do. For the good of the community."

The mouse scampered out to the scarecrow and drew himself up to his full height of four inches. "You there, scarecrow!" he shouted. "Have you heard that the King of Heaven is coming here tonight?"

"Yes, yes, I've heard," said the scarecrow. He was surprised that the mouse would stop and speak to him. Usually the animals acted as if he were not there, and the birds flew over his head and called him names.

"I have been appointed as a neighborhood committee," said the mouse. This was a slight exaggeration, but the mouse thought it made his visit sound official.

"You must be very proud," said the scarecrow.

"It's nothing, really," said the mouse. "What I've been appointed for is to ask you something."

"There's something I'd like to ask you," said the scarecrow. "I've never seen a king. Do you know what He'll look like?"

"Of course," said the mouse. "He'll look like a king. He'll be wearing a golden crown."

"I was afraid I might not know Him when He comes," said the scarecrow.

"You didn't imagine He might be coming out here to see you, did you?" The mouse laughed. "You don't even have a soul. What I've come to ask you is this: Couldn't you lie down where you won't be seen till the King's gone? We all think that would improve the neighborhood."

The scarecrow did not answer. He was hurt but he did not let his hurt show. He just stood stiff and straight and silently shook his head.

"No? Then at least you could plump out that hat and straighten that coat. And that straw sticking out of your sleeves"—the mouse tugged at his own sleek fur cuffs—"I know we can't all look like mice, but you could neaten that a bit, couldn't you, old stick?" And with that the mouse darted away and left the scarecrow to its usual contemplation of its own unimportance.

The afternoon waned slowly into evening, and the evening darkened quietly into night. Time always passes slowly when you are waiting, especially when you are waiting for something important. But the darkness deepened as it always does, a few great stars began to glimmer, and at last the deep vault of the sky so blazed with stars no one could count them all.

Then the dog came running back breathlessly. "Someone is coming, someone is coming!" he barked.

"Is it the King? Is it the King?" all the creatures asked.

"I hardly think so," said the dog, "unless the King is a woman."

"You silly dog," said the owl, "everyone knows the King is never a woman. When a woman is king, she is queen."

In a few minutes, slowly down the road into the valley came the woman the dog had seen. She seemed to be an ordinary woman except for one extraordinary thing: she carried a baby in her arms. She walked very slowly as if she were very tired, and she looked worn and threadbare as if she had come a long way.

When the woman came to the field where the animals were waiting for the King, the ox barred her way.

"Dear ox," said the woman, "my baby and I are tired. We have made a long journey and been turned away at many doors, and now I don't know where to turn. Perhaps you creatures of the field and wood will let us stay with you. All we would ask is a corner in the hay where we might find shelter for the night."

But the ox did not budge. Instead he tossed his huge horned head and let out a gruff bellow as if to say, "Madam, there is no room for you here.'' So the woman turned sadly away.

But out in the farthest field she saw the scarecrow. So she made her way to him. ''Dear scarecrow,'' she said, ''my baby and I are tired, for we have made a long journey. Would you mind if we rested beside you for a moment before we went on? For we can find no shelter anywhere this night.''

The scarecrow hardly knew what to say. Obviously this was not the King everyone was expecting; that King would not be here asking for a place to rest and calling him ''dear scarecrow.'' Nobody had ever called him ''dear scarecrow'' before. He liked it. It sent a warm feeling through him. ''I don't think I'm much of a resting place,'' he said, ''and even less of a shelter. But what I have I'm glad to share with you.''

''Thank you,'' said the woman, and letting herself slip wearily down upon the ground, she leaned her head against his straw-filled rags and pressed herself and her child as close to him as she could.

All the other creatures of the valley had been watching. They had hoped that the woman and her baby would go on.

''That's all we need,'' they told one another, ''a couple of homeless vagrants. When the King comes and sees that, He'll know this isn't the kind of place He'll want to be stopping.''

''At least,'' said the ox, ''we can be glad she's with the scarecrow. They're out in the farthest field and they make a threadbare pair. If the King does notice them, maybe He'll just think they're a family of scarecrows.''

All the creatures laughed loudly at this and soon put the woman and baby out of their minds as they kept watching for the King to come.

It was a strange experience for the scarecrow: a woman crouched at his feet with a baby in her arms. He felt a deep sense of oneness with them; he even felt a little necessary. He had never felt that before.

''You must feel cold,'' he said.

''I do feel cold. But it's not myself that worries me, it's my baby,'' said the woman, hugging him closer to her. ''If only I had something warm to wrap him in.''

''The sheep have warm coats of wool,'' said the scarecrow. ''Perhaps if you would ask them, they would give you a little.''

''Thank you,'' said the mother. So she went to the sheep where they waited for the King. ''Dear sheep,'' she said, ''my baby is cold and I have nothing to wrap him in.'' She held him out in her arms. ''You have such warm coats of wool. Would you please give me a little wool to wrap my baby in?''

"That would be impossible,'' said the old bellwether, who was the spokesman for the herd. "We are expecting an important visitor tonight. Naturally we all want to look our best for Him, and we can't do that if we give away our wool. What is more, if we have any wool to give, it's to Him we will be giving it.''

So the woman went back to the scarecrow. "I was afraid that's how it might be,'' said the scarecrow. "You can understand how they feel, for they want to be as beautiful as they can be on such a night as this. But I have this old coat and hat. They are ragged, but they are clean and fresh, for the wind and rain have washed and winnowed them many times. You can wrap your baby in these.''

"But you would have nothing to cover you with against the cold,'' said the mother.

"Cold and warm—they are one to me,'' said the scarecrow. "I don't feel either. And as for this hat and coat, they are old and tattered. I would feel honored if you would wrap your baby in them.''

The woman hesitated. But then she saw how cold her baby was. So she took off the scarecrow's hat and coat and wrapped her baby in them.

"Thank you, dear scarecrow,'' she said. She sat for a long while rocking her baby in her arms, and she sang him lullabies.

As the scarecrow watched and listened, a strange thing happened. First of all, he did feel cold; the black night air sent a damp chill through him. That surprised him. But then, very quickly he felt warm, and this surprised him, too. A gentle warmth spread through his whole being. It was not a warmth such as he might have felt from the sun beating down on him. This warmth seemed to start at the center of his being and spread outward from himself. For some reason the scarecrow found himself feeling happier than he ever had before in all his life.

But after a while the woman stopped singing and looked again at the scarecrow. "I have been making a long journey, carrying my baby in my arms all night, and I am very tired,'' she said. "If only I had some place to lay him down, I could have a little rest. But the ground is cold and damp, and I have nothing to lay him on.''

"The birds have fluffy coats of down,'' said the scarecrow. "Perhaps if you will ask them for a little down to lay your baby on,

they will give it to you."

"Thank you," said the woman. So she went to the birds where they waited for the King.

"Dear birds," she said, "I have made a long journey and I have carried my baby in my arms all the way." She held him out to them. "Now I am too tired to hold him longer, but I have nowhere to lay him. You have such fluffy coats of down. Would you please give me a little down to lay my baby on?"

"That would be impossible," said the owl, whom all the other birds had appointed to be their night spokesman. "We are expecting an important visitor tonight. Naturally we all want to look our best for Him, and we can't do that if we give away our down. What is more, if we have any down to give, it's to Him we wish to be giving it."

So the mother went sadly back to the scarecrow.

"I was afraid that's how it might be," said the scarecrow. "You can understand how they feel, for they want to be as beautiful as they can be, especially tonight. But I have this straw tied to the ends of my arms and heaped around my post. It is clean and soft. You can lay your baby in my straw."

"But you have already given me your coat and hat, and if I take your straw, what will you have left?" said the woman.

"Rags and straw—what are these?" said the scarecrow. "I would feel honored if you would lay your baby in my straw."

The woman hesitated, but then she felt how tired her arms were. So she took the straw from the ends of the scarecrow's arms and from around his post, and in the straw she laid her son.

"Thank you, dear scarecrow," she said. Then she herself lay down, snuggled her baby in her arms, and fell asleep.

Now the scarecrow stood stripped and stark, a naked cross against the night, but again a strange thing happened. Once more he felt the cold settle through him, this time deeper and more dismaying. But as he watched the woman and her baby sleeping at his feet, the cold passed and the warmth that he had felt before spread through him again. The scarecrow did not know what the warmth was, but it was far the most wonderful feeling he had ever felt. Considering the plight I'm in, and this woman and her baby are in, I don't know why I should feel so happy, he thought; but he did.

The woman did not sleep long. For the night grew deeper and deeper and colder and colder, and in a little while she woke. The scarecrow saw that she was shivering and the child was shivering, too.

"Dear little mother," said the scarecrow, "you must warm yourselves or you may die. The trees have many long branches. Perhaps if you will ask them, they will give you a few branches so that you can build a fire."

"Thank you," said the mother. So she went to the trees where they waited for the King. "Dear trees," she said, "my baby is cold and so am I, and unless we have a fire to warm ourselves we may not be alive when morning comes." She held out her baby in her arms. "You have so many long branches. Would you please give me a little wood so that I can build a fire?"

"That would be impossible," said the oak, who was the spokesman for the grove. "We are expecting an important visitor tonight. Naturally we all want to look our best for Him, and we can't do that if we give away our branches. What is more, if we have any wood to give, it's to Him we intend to be giving it."

So the woman went back once more to the scarecrow.

"I was afraid that's how it might be," said the scarecrow. "You can understand how they feel. For they do want to look as beautiful as they can. But I have this post and this crosspiece; they are good wood, dry and seasoned. They will make a fine, warm fire."

"Scarecrow, dear scarecrow," said the woman, "I have taken your ragged coat and hat and your little pile of straw, and now you have nothing left but this. If I take your post and your crosspiece, you will have nothing left at all."

"I never had much more than nothing," said the scarecrow, "even at my most."

"But have you thought what it is like to burn?" said the woman.

"As to that, you need give it no thought," said the scarecrow. "What have you here but two old pieces of dry wood? The fire is all they are good for. But if you don't have a fire, neither you nor your son will live to see the morning."

The woman hesitated. But when she felt her baby shivering, she did as the scarecrow bade. She took a little of his straw and lit it. It burst into flame quickly.

When the woman lifted the post and crosspiece to lay them in the fire, the strange warmth that the scarecrow had felt before spread through him again, this time even stronger.

"When you took my hat and coat and when you took my straw,"

said the scarecrow, "I felt a strange feeling. And now I feel it once more, this time even stronger. It is a very warm feeling and a very beautiful feeling. The warmth starts from the center of my being and radiates out until it fills me. It radiates out even beyond myself, so that I become more than I have ever been, one with you and your baby, and even with all the creatures in the valley, even those who do not like me, and when I feel this warmth, I wish only good for everything that is."

"I know that feeling well," said the woman. "Don't you know what it is?"

The scarecrow shook his head.

"You are feeling love," said the woman.

"If this is love," said the scarecrow, "then love must be the warmest, most beautiful, and most blessed of all the feelings anyone in this world can ever feel. I wish I could feel it forever."

"You can if you will," said the woman.

"The straw is burning," said the scarecrow. "It will go out quickly if you do not feed it with the wood."

"Are you sure you want to do this?" said the woman.

"Quickly, quickly," said the scarecrow.

So the woman laid the post and crosspiece in the fire, and the wood burst into flame, and a fierce pain, more painful than he had ever imagined pain could be, burst through the scarecrow. He started to cry out, but he held back his cry, for he knew that if he cried out in pain, she would put out the fire. Instead he prayed, "Love, love, be with me now!"

Then it seemed to him that love touched the flames that were pain and turned them into flames of love, so that the flames, though they burned, only burned away that which was gross and less than it should be, until all that was left was a radiance and a glow. Then, suddenly, the scarecrow felt nothing at all.

When the other creatures saw the fire, they were at first a little frightened. But when they saw that it was the scarecrow burning, most of them were a little pleased.

"That's good riddance," said one of the starlings.

Then they quickly turned back to watching for the King. For all I know, they may be watching still.

Meanwhile there was much ado in heaven.

The Lord was returning from His journey over earth, and the angels were all atwitter. Sometimes when He came back, He came back depressed. Then the angels knew that He would be prodding them. "We're not doing nearly enough," He would tell them. "Those creatures down there aren't getting the help they need to become what they were made to be."

But sometimes when He came back, He came back rejoicing, for He brought back something beautiful and holy that He had found. Then the angels rejoiced, too.

As the scarecrow made his way up heaven's principal street, he saw the angels looking at him with the same disapproving looks and muttering the same disapproving mutters as the valley creatures had. He felt a little frightened.

"How did that get in here?" said one angel.

"Isn't there anyone keeping the gate?" said another.

And the third angel said: "That can't be a scarecrow. They don't have a soul."

But suddenly the angel faces changed.

The sour sneers blossomed into smiles and the ugly mutters burst into hallelujahs of awe and exultation.

Then the scarecrow sensed that he was not walking alone. Someone was walking beside him and had thrown an arm around him, an arm that filled him with the same strange warmth that he had felt before.

The scarecrow was afraid to turn and look at the figure that strode beside him, for he knew from the expression on the angels' faces, it must be One of transcendent glory.

And he knew that something strange and wonderful was happening because when he looked down at himself, he saw not sticks and straw and rags, but a shining glory, too.

At last he stole a glance. What he saw he could not say, for who can say what He looks like? All he could say was that he had come very close to Truth and found that it was Love. For the Truth that is Love had on his ragged scarecrow hat but wore it like a crown, and his ragged scarecrow coat, but now it was a King's robe!

Then the scarecrow, too, began to sing hallelujahs.

An Event of Major Importance

THE STORY I am about to relate is only the beginning of a story. It's about the birth of a child, and you can't get much more at the beginning than that. For thousands of years human beings are going to be talking and writing about this birth and this child. I believe that this birth occurred now because we are at the beginning of a new age, the age of Aquarius, and this child has a special role to play in this age. When you hear the details, I think you will believe this, too.

I don't imagine anyone will ever have all the details. I have tried to find everyone who was connected with the event, and to put down what he had to say about what happened, so that we can get as complete a picture as possible.

Most events like this go unrecorded until long after they have occurred. Then usually all we have is someone's unsubstantiated, often sketchy, often fanciful tale. That's why I don't want this to be just my story. I want it to be the story of all those who had any part in the event. I don't care how small a part.

For instance, I called on the director of the hospital. In our time every child is born in a hospital. And since this child wasn't, and there was a hospital nearby, I wanted to find out why.

The hospital was one of those little community hospitals you find in rural areas, the kind several towns go together to build. I called the director on the telephone. He said he didn't know anything about a mother-to-be being turned away, but finally he reluctantly agreed to an interview.

"After you called me," he said when I came, "I naturally made inquiries. We are here to serve everyone. I've talked to the young woman who was on the reception desk the night this fellow you describe came in and asked if he could bring in his wife. The hospital was full, and that's what she told the man."

When I asked the director if it really was that full, the director snapped angrily: "Certainly it was. I've checked myself. Every room was occupied. That's not an unusual condition. We're the only hospital in this area, and we're not a big city facility.

"And this fellow was a stranger here. When the young woman asked him where he lived, he said he was just traveling through. You have to admit, that wasn't much of an answer. She asked him if he had hospital insurance, and of course he didn't."

When I asked whether you had to have insurance to get in the hospital, he snapped again: "No, of course you don't. The young woman was just following instructions when she asked him that. We ask everyone that, that's natural, isn't it?"

"Isn't there always room in the hospital in an emergency?" I asked.

"If we know it's an emergency," said the director. "We didn't know that. The man didn't bring his wife in. So the young woman on the desk had no chance to see how far along she was. For all she knew, the woman might not be having the baby for a week."

No, he said, he had made a full investigation, and the receptionist had done exactly the right thing. There was no room in the hospital and she had told him that.

I thanked the director and asked if it was all right for me to talk to the receptionist. He was irritated, but he said it would be all right.

Her story was much like his. This young man had come in, dressed in blue jeans. He had long hair and a beard, but she had rather liked him. He was clean. No, he hadn't talked rough or threatened her or anything. In fact, he was soft-spoken and seemed rather shy. As she'd said, he seemed nice enough. But there was simply nothing she could do. She hadn't liked turning him away. She didn't like turning anyone away. She had been uneasy enough to follow him to the door and look out when he left. He'd climbed into an old beat-up Volkswagen van with shabby curtains at the window. "You know," she said, "the kind all these young hippies live in. You see them on the roads every day."

Why was I asking about it? she wanted to know. Was he a friend of mine? Had something bad happened? Were they suing the hospital or something?

I told her no, nothing bad had happened. They had had their baby, and everything was fine.

"I'm glad to hear that," she said. "I'm sorry I had to turn them away. But there was nothing else I could do. You can see that."

I said, "Yes, I can see."

You probably want to know how I got involved in this. It was the star that aroused my interest.

I say star, though the astronomers said it was a comet. That is typical of this whole affair. Was it a star, was it a comet, was it anything? Maybe you remember—it was in the papers briefly—a kind of nine-day wonder. A French astronomer named Bertrand discovered the comet, and the papers announced that astronomers were predicting that it was going to be the most glorious sight the heavens had

produced in centuries. But instead of growing brighter, as was predicted, the heavenly visitor seemed to fade, at least as far as most people were concerned. Because when I asked people whether they had seen it, they would look at me, surprised, and say, "What comet?" or, "Is there a comet up there?" or, "Where is it supposed to be?" The papers finally announced that the comet was a fizzle, and gave a long scientific explanation of how this had happened.

But the strange thing is that it was not a fizzle—not, that is, for me. I saw it. And instead of fading, night by night it got brighter and brighter. Not only did it get brighter, I had the strange feeling it was drawing nearer. Yes, the light was slowly moving across the sky, and every night it was moving nearer to me than the night before. The phenomenon fascinated me. So much so that I wrote to Bertrand.

How come, I asked Bertrand, he had discovered a comet that was supposed to be the most glorious sight in the heavens, and there it was as glorious as he had said it would be—except that nobody saw it except me (though I didn't think it looked like a comet)? What's more, whatever it was, I was absolutely certain its light was moving across the sky and every night was coming nearer to where I was.

To my pleasant surprise, Bertrand fired a letter back immediately. He was very much interested that I could see his comet, because he continued to see it, too. One of his fellow astronomers had written to him that he saw it. But apparently we three were the only ones who could see it. Why this was, he had no idea. As to whether it was a comet, he had reluctantly concluded it was not, at least in the ordinary sense of comets. A heavenly visitor, to be sure, but not just a chance wanderer from outer space.

"You probably think I am crazy," I wrote, "but the idea has grown in me that this light is a kind of celestial beacon in a giant hand, beckoning those who see it to follow it. It is not only a light sent to shine on earth, it is shining on one particular spot on earth. What is more, unless my powers of observation are very distorted, that spot is not far from where I live."

Bertrand wrote back that he did not think I was crazy. He and his astronomer friend had slowly come to the same conclusion. They had been independently tracking the motion of the light and computing its course. If their computations were correct, when in a few days the light was closest to the earth, it would be shining on some point on the earth's surface that was within a hundred miles of the city where I lived. To find the exact spot on which the light was falling would require a ground search.

He and his colleague were so sure of what they had discovered, and so sure that an event of major importance in the history of the globe was occurring, that the two of them were flying into my city and hoped I would be available to lead them in their search.

I immediately wired back that I was eagerly awaiting their coming and since I had a large house, I expected them to be my guests.

So in a few days the three of us were driving out into the country, searching for an object on which a strange light was falling that only we could see.

I wish I could give you here all our conversations. They were profoundly interesting, but they would unnecessarily prolong this tale. I have, however, carefully written them down and am preserving them. There is no question in my mind that a drama has unfolded here of paramount importance to humankind, and future generations will be probing for every morsel of information connected with it.

Our search turned out to be more difficult than I had imagined it would be.

For one thing, it had to be conducted by night, when the light was visible. My two friends were expert at observing heavenly bodies and computing directions and distances. But the light was up in the sky and the point we were searching for was down on the ground, and to reach it we had no direct route. By night we had to follow country roads that wound through many miles of woods and fields, up and down hills and over streams.

And of course, part of what made it hard was that we didn't have the slightest idea what we were looking for. Even when we found it, we could hardly believe that was what we had been looking for—a newborn child in a Volkswagen van! Who could dream that such an ordinary event could be so momentous as to call for such an extraordinary celestial phenomenon! But there could be no doubt, when at last we located it: the star was directly overhead and the light was shining straight down, enveloping the van like a mantle.

I had thought that my friends and I were probably the only ones to know about the event, but the father of the child told me that on the night the child was born, several people who lived on farms in the vicinity had come to the van. Naturally I went looking for them. At the fourth farm where I stopped, as I questioned the man, he became very excited and called his wife into the room, and between them they blurted out quite a tale.

They had gone to bed early, but about three in the morning they awoke, for their room was full of light. They rose and looked out the window. They whole sky was aglow. They had never seen anything like it before.

At first they thought something must be on fire, for the light seemed to rise and fall in great waves. They threw on some clothes and ran out into the yard. But the light was not from a fire. It was hard to describe, they said. The woman said it was a little like a night when the moon is full and the sky is cloudy and the moon rides the clouds, passing in and out of sight as if it were riding the swells of a sea. But she knew that wasn't what it was.

There were no clouds, there was just this pulsing, dancing, swirling light, swinging all around them.

I tried to tell them about the comet.

The light they saw, they insisted, was no comet. Or star either. They could see the stars, they were all up there as usual. But this light was down around them. It was as if the air were full of light.

"One time long ago," said the man, "I came out suddenly on a cliff's edge above a lake, and below me was a great flock of snow geese. I was right over them before they saw me and rose. They swept up and around me in a vast rush, almost brushing my face. For a moment my world was wings, driving, swooping, thrusting wings, so that I was almost swept up with them. That's the way it was that night, except that it was lights."

His wife looked at me strangely. "It was angels," she said. "Angels, that's what it was."

The man nodded his head.

"We heard the music and the voices," she said.

"There were voices?" I said.

"Music and voices," said the man.

The music, they said, was as hard to describe as the light. But it was the most beautiful music they had ever listened to. They went to the Methodist Church, and sometimes when the organ was playing and the whole congregation was singing, it sounded pretty good. But that was nothing compared to this. It wasn't gospel music, and it wasn't country music. But somehow it made them feel like praying and praising and leaping up and dancing all at the same time.

Then they began to hear the words. Over and through and above that music came words.

The woman went out of the room and came back with a scrap of paper that she held out to me. "I wrote the words down," she said, "so we wouldn't forget."

I asked the woman if she would give me the paper. I have put it away with my conversations with my astronomer friends for future publication.

These were the words on the scrap of paper:

"God has lit His candle in the night, and His candle is the Spirit in man. God is and He is good, and His will is life and peace and joy. This day He has given out of His love a child who will be a blessing to all the world.

"Do not be afraid, but rise and seek, and you will find nearby a man and a woman, and in the arms of the woman a newborn child, and when you look upon the child, you will behold God, and you will kneel down and lift up your heart in praises."

"We were afraid, " said the man, "but not too afraid. We went across our yard, out the gate, down the road, until we came to that van. The moment we saw it, we knew that's where the lights and music and voices wanted us to go. And sure enough, there were the father and mother and newborn child. And when we saw the child, we knew we beheld God, and we fell down on our knees and gave praises."

I talked to the father and mother of the child. Or was he the father? I suppose it depends on how you look at it.

They were slow to talk to me, but with the story they had to tell, I guess they had to pour it out to somebody, and they could see I was their friend and believed them, incredible as their story was.

(The two astronomers and I had pitched in and given them a gift. "The baby is going to need some things," we said.)

So the young man finally told me how they had come from a little town in another part of the country, where they had known each other all their life. They had been sweethearts since they were in the fourth grade; he had decided then she was the most beautiful girl he had ever seen, and he had never changed his mind. He couldn't remember a time when he hadn't taken for granted that they were going to get married.

You can imagine, then, what he felt like when one day she came to

him and said, "I'm going to have a baby."

"For God's sake, whose?" he asked her.

She just shook her head.

"I had never touched her," he told me. "I just had taken for granted that some day she'd be my wife, and then. . . ."

"I love you," she said. "I have never loved anyone else, and I never will."

"Whose baby is it?" he said.

When she just shook her head again, he had turned and left her. He felt there was only one course he could take, and that was to get out of town. He couldn't bear the humiliation that would be his when his woman—the only woman he'd ever had—had a baby by somebody else. He had this Volkswagen van, so he packed his things to leave.

But as he tried to drive away, he realized how much he was in love. She was his woman, the only woman he had ever loved, the only woman he could even imagine wanting for his wife. The longer he thought about it, the more certain he became that he loved her just as much as he ever had, and would never love anybody else.

So he turned around and went back. "You say you love me and have never loved anybody else," he said to her.

"I love you, and have never loved anybody else, and never will," she said.

"Then marry me," he said. "I love you, and will never love anybody else, and that's all that matters. I don't care whose baby it is."

"No, wait," she said. "I have to tell you something. You'll think I'm crazy, but you've got to believe what I have to tell you, or I can't marry you. I just can't."

What she told him was that months ago she had a dream. In the dream something came to her. She couldn't say what it was. It was just a—a presence. But it was an overwhelming sense of a presence. And it filled her with itself in a way she couldn't describe. It just made her its own.

And she heard voices that told her: "You have been filled with life and you have conceived and will bear the child of life. You are blessed above all women, and through the child you have conceived all human beings will be blessed."

"I know it all sounds crazy," the young father told me. "But that's what happened. It was past my power to understand, but she said she had had no man, and if she said that, I knew it had to be true. Yet there she was, pregnant. It was hard to believe it could just be a dream.

"But I said to her, 'We are going to be married.' And we were.

"I knew the best thing for us would be to get out of town. So we took off in this van. And here we are. I still don't know what it's all about. And it's still hard to believe. But obviously something has happened. Something that isn't just a dream.

"There's this light in the sky that's followed us; you say that's how you found us. And the night the baby was born, there were all those—do you believe they really could be angels?" He shook his head incredulously.

"I believe," I said.

I'm not sure how to describe the young mother except to say I liked her. The night I talked to her, she was dressed in a plain dark dress that looked like it had had a lot of wear. She had dark hair and dark eyes. Her eyes were the most outstanding thing about her. They were very large, very soft, very gentle, very deep. Have you ever looked into anyone's eyes and thought you were looking into a very deep well? Her eyes were like that.

"I don't know what to tell you," she said to me. "What can I say? It would be easier, more understandable, for me to say that the baby was someone's other than my husband's, except that it isn't. It still sounds unbelievable, even to me. But the way he told you, that's the way it happened. I realized I was going to have a baby. But I had never been with a man, not even with my husband whom I love. Yet I was going to have a child. I had had all those dreams, or visions, or whatever they were. There were lots of them. I would wake, or at least I thought I was awake, and I would lie there in my bed, more afraid than anything else. Because I had the sense that I was not alone. Yet I never actually saw anything. And I'm not sure I heard anything either. At least, I'm not sure I ever heard a real voice speaking out. But it was like a voice, just as it was like a presence. And the voice said, 'You are with child, but don't be afraid, for your child is meant for great things, and is the offspring of life itself.'

"Oh, I felt all sorts of things in those nights . . . fear, shame, pride, pain, ecstasy! But slowly I came to feel that whatever it was, it was good.

"Was it God? Was it the Holy Spirit? Was it an angel? It never gave itself a name. I wish I could remember now all the things I thought I experienced, all the things I thought I heard, all the things I thought I felt. But very shortly it gets hard to remember exactly. It's so real when it occurs, and afterward it's like a dream or something you read. That's the way it is now.

"But I have a child. The child is real.

"Sometimes I think I've gone out of my mind; this can't have happened. But it has happened. I don't know why, but I know, I know in the depths of my being, I've been chosen in a very special way to be the mother of a very special child, who is going to bring a blessing to all the world."

* * *

I've tried to put down here just what the mother said. That has not been easy because it wasn't so much what she said, as it was the way she said it. While I was listening to her, there was no doubt in my mind that she was telling me the truth. She had had an unbelievable, soul-exalting experience. This young girl was no longer just a young girl. She had encountered something beyond her power or mine to understand, and she had been transformed and transfigured.

I have met a number of very creative people who have had great creative moments. But as I stood before this mother, I knew that I was in the presence of someone who had had a creative experience on the very highest level of being. There was no more doubt in my mind than in hers that the child she had borne had a meaning for all of us, and a role to play beyond anything any of us could even imagine. As I stood there in the presence of that young woman, I knew that I was privileged to have a small part in an historical occurrence of the first magnitude.

"I have brought forth a baby, a wonderful baby," she said. "My baby—my baby!—is going to be a blessing to all the world."

Then she held the baby out to me.

As to the full meaning of this strange event, as to the exact significance this birth has for humankind, this of course, only the passing years will reveal.

What is my belief about the child?

All I know is that when her mother held her out to me and I looked into her eyes, I fell down and worshiped her.

The Woman Who Learned to Love Christmas

THIS IS A STORY about Christmas. More particularly, it is a story about a woman who did not like Christmas.

Ms. D. Darlington was the assistant to the assistant manager of the city's largest department store. At the store, Christmas was held in higher veneration than mother, the American flag, or even the Annual Red Tag Storewide Sale. So Ms. Darlington did not often say how she felt. She had to think about Christmas a great deal of the time; that made her like it even less. When she did talk about it—far away from the store and among friends—her eyes gleamed and her lips curled.

"To like Christmas you have to like headaches, riots, and traffic jams," she would say with a shudder. "Christmas is hokum, pure hokum. It's supposed to be a holy day, a quiet day when people go to church to worship the newborn Lord. I might buy that. But name one thing about Christmas that has anything to do with that. Name one thing that isn't a fable or a rip-off. Eat too much, drink too much, spend too much—and afterward wish you hadn't—that's Christmas."

Ms. Darlington often talked to herself—that is, when she was not talking to several thousand other people or, to be accurate, when several thousand other people were not talking to her. To make it easier for her to be talked to she wore a pager, and during the Christmas season it beeped incessantly. "Ms. Darlington, will you come to credit, please . . . Ms. Darlington, this is store security . . . Ms. Darlington, hurry, please, hurry to ladies' wear on the fourth floor . . . Ms. Darlington, are you there? . . . Ms. Darlington . . . Ms. Darling . . . Ms. Dar . . . Ms. . . ."

"Ms. Darlington, go to the jewelry counter." She was hurrying through toyland when her pager sounded. As she turned toward the escalator, she spied two little boys putting a toy racing car on the electric train track to see if they could have a train wreck.

With a lunge she snapped up the car before the train reached it. The little boys glared at her, yelled something, then whirled about and ran.

The only thing worse than grown-ups at Christmas is children, she thought. They break the toys or try to steal them, they stop up toilets, get lost, ride the down-escalator up, and the up-escalator down, and monopolize the elevators. Whoever said Christmas is for children is right—they deserve one another.

At the next counter she saw that a little girl had taken out of its box and was fiercely hugging the most expensive doll in the store, the big doll with hair that looked natural and could be set, and skin that felt natural and could be bathed; the doll that talked and cried and drank from a bottle, all naturally, and naturally wet its diaper.

She whisked the doll out of the little girl's arms.

"You're not allowed to handle the dolls," she said. "You'll break her."

"Oh, no, I love her," said the little girl. She was a plain child, with big brown eyes in a pale thin face, and she was dressed in plain, almost threadbare clothes.

"Haven't I had to take this doll away from you before?" said Ms. Darlington.

The little girl nodded.

"I thought so," said Ms. Darlington. "If I catch you touching her again . . . ." But somehow the little girl's big eyes hanging so hungrily on the doll stopped what she was going to say, and she concluded, "Don't you have anyone who could buy her for you?"

"I wish I did," said the little girl. "You'd have to be rich to buy someone like her. She's the most beautiful doll in the world."

Ms. Darlington caught herself starting to say, "Tomorrow's Christmas. Maybe Santa Claus will bring her to you," but she stopped before she began. She was surprised that she would even think of compounding childish illusions by uttering such a falsehood.

"You can't play with the doll," she said sharply. "It's time you were home. It's almost closing time here. Get along." But her voice softened as she spoke, and she found herself giving the little girl a warm pat instead of the rough push she had intended to give her.

I wonder if she'll get anything at all, thought Ms. Darlington as she watched the girl disappear slowly down the aisle. Then she said aloud, "Christmas! What isn't hokum is heartache."

"Not if you find its true meaning," said a voice. "She's already gotten a lot just through wanting it."

"Why, I wager she'll get nothing," snorted Ms. Darlington. She turned with a start. Who could have spoken? She had a strange feeling it was the doll.

But at that moment her pager sounded again. "Ms. Darlington, jewelry needs you immediately."

"I could have sworn that doll spoke. This Christmas nonsense is driving me out of my head," she said as she hurried toward the escalator. As it started down, she looked back. The doll was looking at her, smiling, and the doll said, "No, it's driving you into your

SPECIAL!
REAL WOODEN
CRECHE
SPECIAL TODAY!

heart. There's hope for you, Ms. Darlington."

"I ought to run out of this insane store before I'm carried out screaming 'Merry Christmas!' " she said to herself as the escalator bore her gently toward the lower floor. Softly undulating under her feet, it seemed almost like a haven. "This escalator is the sanest thing in this store—and even it has breakdowns. Christmas! It's not spelled right. The first syllable ought to be *crass* and the second *mess*. Crassmess! That's what it is."

At the jewelry counter she had to make the customer feel that she was always right and at the same time keep the clerk from quitting. Then she went to the lost and found department. Here she found a woman and a child. The woman claimed the child was her sister's and the child just kept screaming, "Mama! I want my mama!" Then she was called to the north entrance where one of the clerks told her that he had just stopped a little boy from eating the ornaments on the big Christmas tree inside the entrance.

For a moment she paused beside the tree. It was a real tree. "We haven't had a real tree in the store for years," the manager had told her. "The customers will love it, a real old-fashioned Christmas kind of thing!"

She had started to tell him how many houses were burned down by Christmas tree fires, but instead she had only smiled and muttered to herself, "Christmas trees were dreamed up by the 'society of firebugs!' " and she decided to increase her secret donation to the environmental group that was seeking a ban on Christmas trees as a waste of our forest resources.

Now as she stood beside it, bathed in its rosiny fragrance, she had to admit that it was a beautiful tree, tall and straight, perfectly shaped, towering to the ceiling, laden with baubles and lights. The green tree suffused a warm and tranquil atmosphere in which for a moment she felt engulfed.

"I thought the manager was nutty to insist on you," she said to the tree. "But I'm glad he did. You're the only natural thing in this store."

"Thank you," said the tree.

She looked at the tree in alarm.

"But that's not entirely true," the tree went on. "You are natural, too."

This can't be happening, she thought. Here I am, Ms. D. Darlington, standing here quietly and calmly, having a conversation with a tree. Christmas has finally done it—I've gone mad.

The tree read her thoughts.

"Because you are talking to a tree?" it said. "You think that's any sillier than talking to most of the people you've been talking to today? I assure you, some of the sanest people the world has ever known have talked to trees. In fact, talking to trees has helped a lot of people to stay sane."

"Nevertheless, one doesn't go around talking to trees," said Ms. Darlington.

"Ordinarily, true. But then trees don't go around talking to people. You looked as if you needed someone to talk to you."

"Perhaps I did, but I didn't expect . . . ."

"The someone to be me, I know. But I needed someone to talk to, too. I don't have much longer to talk, you know. Tomorrow is Christmas, and after that . . . ." The tree sighed.

"I'm sorry," she said.

"Oh, there's nothing to be sorry about," said the tree. "It's been delightful. I've enjoyed the whole affair. Not many trees get to be decked out so beautifully and stand in the main entrance of the main department store in town. I've met everyone of any importance in this town, not formally, but we've brushed against one another."

"But tomorrow you'll be taken down and hauled out in the trash."

"Oh, not tomorrow," said the tree. "Nobody's working tomorrow. Tomorrow will be a quiet day for me—give me time to sort out my thoughts and run through my memories. A lot of lovely things have happened to me in this last month, you know. It will be pleasant to think of them."

"But the day after tomorrow!"

"Everybody has a day after tomorrow," said the tree. "Right now we have the day before Christmas."

"Christmas! I hate it!"

"So I see," said the tree.

"But look what it does. It covers you with baubles and decorations, and then . . . ."

"Baubles and decorations, aren't they lovely?" said the tree.

"They're flimflam and fakery! There's nothing real about Christmas."

"I'm real," said the tree. "So are you."

"That's the worst thing about Christmas—what it does to the real things. It's made me a nervous wreck, and it's torn you out of the forest where you might be living a beautiful natural life."

"I might have grown to be a forest giant," said the tree reflectively, "but only a few of us trees end up that way. Most of us end up as match sticks or paper plates or yesterday's newspaper."

"But you might have lived for a thousand years!"

"Maybe so," said the tree. "But the purpose of life is not to survive, but to live while you survive. And I have lived! I have been beautiful, I have been admired, I have been the center of great excitement. No, I will always be thankful for Christmas."

"But it's killed you!"

"Ah, no, it has let me live," said the tree, "and if you let it, it will do the same for you."

Suddenly Ms. Darlington became aware that her pager was beeping furiously. "Ms. Darlington, Ms. Darlington, are you there, Ms. Darlington? Will you come to the south entrance, please?"

When she reached the south entrance, she found no one there except the usual swirl of people passing in and out of the revolving doors. At this entrance, instead of a tree there was a Santa seated in a beautiful red sleigh drawn by eight reindeer, all constructed out of some new kind of marvelous plastic.

Ms. Darlington found herself drawn to stare at this Santa. As she did, she found him staring at her. She felt a little annoyed. "If I didn't know this Santa was plastic, I'd swear he was looking at me. A very talented artist must have worked for weeks to create such a lifelike effect. And on such nonsense. What a waste Christmas is!"

At that moment Santa winked. "That's nonsense!" he said. "So you finally got here, Ms. Darlington. I've been paging you for the last five minutes. What took you so long?"

"I—I was talking to a Christmas tree," she said. The moment she said it, she wished she hadn't, it sounded so ridiculous. But then she realized that it sounded no more ridiculous than to be talking to a Santa.

"I can understand that," said Santa. "I hope the conversation was enlightening. I've known some highly intelligent Christmas trees."

"This can't be happening to me," she said to herself. "I know—I haven't really come to the store today, I'm still in bed—I'm just dreaming all this."

"No, you are not in bed. You are not dreaming. You are standing in the south entrance of this department store talking to me, Santa Claus."

"This is absurd," said Ms. Darlington. "In the first place, there isn't any Santa Claus, and even if there were, you're just a display model made for the store—out of papier-mâché or plastic or something."

"Let's settle for something," said Santa Claus. "We are all made out of something, aren't we?"

"But I'm real—flesh and blood," she said.

"Faugh! Is flesh and blood anything but a special kind of plastic? That's not what makes you real. There are a lot of people running around this store who aren't very real and a lot of things for sale here that are."

"But you are just a—just a—Santa."

"Is there anything more real than that?" said Santa. "Oh, I know what you think—Santa is make-believe. But surely you've learned by now that make-believe for most people is the most real thing about them. Far more real than outer events. Most people wouldn't be alive at all if they didn't have their make-believes. Aren't you mainly make-believe, Ms. Darlington?"

Ms. Darlington looked at herself as if to disavow it.

"Oh, it's not what you're looking at that makes you real, Ms. Darlington. It's all those hopes and dreams and expectations and imaginings that crowd your mind. So I am the work of imagination. Do you think you are not, my dear?"

"It's not at all the same thing," said Ms. Darlington indignantly. She wondered what she was doing here, arguing with a plastic Santa Claus. Perhaps arguing with a Christmas tree had made it easier.

"How do you know it's not the same thing," said Santa, "since you don't know what I am like? In fact, you say you don't even think I *am*. Isn't that true?"

"Well, I do find it hard to . . ." she said doubtfully.

"Ho, ho, ho! Let's make it easier. Step over here a little closer."

Ms. Darlington found herself edging toward the sleigh.

"Fine, my dear. Here, get right in the sleigh with me. There's plenty of room."

"Oh, I can't do that," she said. But to her amazement she found herself climbing into the sleigh and settling comfortably down on the seat beside the white-bearded, red-robed figure who quietly but expertly wrapped around her the blanket that lay beside him. It was the warmest, softest, dreamiest blanket she had ever snuggled into. The moment its folds fell around her she found herself curling down, not only into the midst of the blanket, but into the midst of herself.

"Wonderful, we're off," shouted Santa. "Come, Vixen and Dancer and Cupid and Comet! Come, Donder and Blitzen and Dasher and Prancer!" He turned to her with a twinkle. "Sorry, Rudolph is not with us this evening. He is the work of someone else's imagination."

Santa had no sooner spoken than the reindeer sprang into action, and before you could say, "Merry Christmas!" they were jolting across—she was not sure what.

"Where—where are we going?" she asked breathlessly.

"On my usual journey, of course, dear. It's Christmas Eve, you know, and already moving toward morning in some parts of the earth. The people are waiting for me. I try to get around to all of them."

She could see the breath of the reindeer floating back in frozen puffs, making a kind of Christmas fantail behind the sleigh. As they sped along, Santa kept reaching into his sack and casting things out.

She shook her head in disbelief. "Then you really do make a midnight journey giving gifts to everyone?"

"I try," said Santa. "Some won't let me in—though I only need a very small chink, you know."

"I—I haven't believed in you."

"I know," said Santa. "There are people who don't believe in George Washington or God."

"I—I thought you were an invention of Madison Avenue or the National Retail Merchants Association."

"I am an invention," said Santa. "But much older than that. I know I'm used to promote sales and entice customers to come into the store. But even before there were stores, I was the invention of man's desire to believe that there is a spirit in him and in the world that is kind and generous and selfless, and leaves no one out."

"But people are left out," she said.

"All the more need for my being," said Santa. "If the Christmas spirit is to touch everyone, it is going to have to take many shapes. I am one of those shapes. But not the least, I hope. I feel that I bring happiness, or at least a happy expectation, to many—and if most of

DOLL
GIRL DOLL

them are children that is no small accomplishment, for are we not all children at heart? So even to those who are no longer children I may bring a sigh of remembrance of a childhood long forgotten, or at least a chuckle as they hurry by—and that, too, is no mean accomplishment."

The ride was not at all like anything she might have imagined it would be. She would have thought it would be a smooth and gentle glide across a starlit or perhaps a snow-filled sky.

It was a jolting ride. The sleigh soared, sometimes as in a flash. It lost elevation as quickly as it rose, sucking out her breath. It rolled from side to side. It pitched and tossed. It passed through long stretches of darkness and long stretches of emptiness. At times she had a sense of shooting up over frigid peaks. At times she had a sense of skimming over stormy seas. They passed through rainstorms; the raindrops tasted like tears. They passed through hailstorms; when the hail struck, it stung like angry words. They passed through sounds like crying and sounds like laughter. They passed through silences that were peaceful and through silences that were dread.

"Where are we now?" she asked.

"Somewhere between fear and hope, somewhere between doubt and resolution," said Santa.

"But are we passing over New York or London or some little village? Where on earth are we?"

"Earth? We're not on earth at all."

"You—you don't travel over earth, landing on people's rooftops and sliding down their chimneys?"

"You really thought it might be like that? I suppose Clement Moore's poem is responsible for that idea. I don't blame you for not believing that sort of thing. It would be impossible, wouldn't it? But it has been fun for children."

"But if we're not traveling through the sky, where are we traveling?"

"Where would you expect someone like me to be traveling? The sky's for birds and airplanes. And I'm hardly either. There's only one place I've ever made my trip. That is through human hearts. I wouldn't last a minute anywhere else."

"Then it's human hearts I've been taking this ride through?"

"Human hearts!"

"But it's been so wild!"

"You wouldn't expect a trip through human hearts to be like a slow train ride, would you? Think of your own heart."

Suddenly she felt frightened. "Don't we ever stop?"

"When you have to visit every person in the world in one night, you don't have much time for pausing along the way. Do you need to stop?"

"Yes, yes, I think I do."

Even as she spoke, they had stopped. They were in a small room. It was simply furnished.

"Why, this is the room I had when I was a little girl," said Ms. Darlington.

Santa nodded.

"Is—is it Christmas Eve?"

"We wouldn't be here if it wasn't," said Santa.

"But there are no decorations."

"I thought you didn't believe in wasting money on such foolish frivolities."

"I don't see a tree. I always had a tree."

Santa looked at her curiously. "Did you? But is it not a pagan custom—and a fire hazard, too?"

"And gifts—where are the gifts? My parents gave me gifts."

"But would you add to the cheap commercialism of the times?"

Ms. Darlington looked at the little girl. "And she—is she—?"

Slowly the little girl raised her head. Her face was not a young face, but had a dry, tight look; hard lines were beginning to form around the mouth and eyes. She was crying. She looked as if she had been crying for a long time.

Ms. Darlington let out a long sigh of relief. "I thought it might be . . . who is she?"

"You don't recognize her?"

She shook her head.

"Look again," said Santa. "You know her very well."

Ms. Darlington began to feel a strange panic. "It's not me, it's not!" she cried. "I didn't look at all like that when I was a little girl."

At that the little girl let out a tremendous sob, and looked at her accusingly.

"Of course you didn't," said Santa. "She's not the little girl you were, she's the little girl you *are*."

Suddenly Ms. Darlington realized that she was not sitting in the sleigh, but standing alongside it. She was crying, crying as if her heart were broken.

"I've helped you as much as I can," said Santa. "Now you need more help than I can give you. There's only one place in the store where you may be able to find it. I suggest you try Christmas decorations."

When she reached Christmas decorations, she saw no one there. "I wonder why he sent me here?" she said.

Then she heard a soft voice, "Are you looking for me, Ms. Darlington?"

She looked around. "Where are you?"

"Right over here," said the voice.

"I don't see you," she said.

"Many people haven't been able to," said the voice. "You have to want to very much."

Ms. Darlington's eyes followed the voice to a small wooden crèche on the next counter.

"Are you in the crèche?" she asked.

"Can you think of a better place for me to be on Christmas Eve?" said the voice. She realized that it was the Holy Child lying in the manger who was speaking. "I hear you don't care much for this merry Christmas mix of worldliness and wonder."

"Well, I . . . ."

"I had to get used to it myself," said the Child. "But when you look aright at it, you see that it fits the occasion very well. After all, it is my birthday, and birthdays ought to be gala!"

"But you—you get lost in it all!"

"Oh, the form perhaps, but not the spirit! Christmas is a spirit! I am the shape it took two thousand years ago in a village in Judea, but I was old before I was born. You can find me almost anywhere, if you look. If you can't, you haven't found me at all. Let my old friends tell you how they did it."

"You have to put your heart into it," said the donkey who was standing by the manger. "I'm only a donkey, but I found Christmas. I carried Christmas on my back that night, and I found that when the burden you bear is love, it is not you who bears love, it is love that bears you."

"You have to give a little," said the ox. "The sheep and I gave

Christmas our stable and straw. And we found that when you give with no thought of return, the gift you have given does not leave you less, but makes you more."

"You have to let it grow in you," said Mary. "I carried it next to my heart for a long time. I found that to do the will of life, even when the way seems frightening and strange, is to become what you were meant to be, and that is always something gloriously beautiful."

"I was the least important part of the story," said Joseph. "Oh, I'm there, but who gives me much thought? But I did what was mine to do, even when I didn't want to do it. So I found that there are no unimportant parts. If the least did not do the little things that are theirs to do, the great events would never take place."

Then the angels began to sing. Ms. Darlington had never heard a song like theirs. She did not understand the words—they were singing in an unknown tongue—but she understood the music, for it lifted her heart.

I've never believed in angels, she thought.

"You've not believed in many things," said an angel. "But surely even an unbeliever must believe that the world has wonders in it beyond his conceiving. To find your sense of wonder is to find Christmas."

"We shepherds found Christmas when we heard that angel song," said a shepherd. "Shepherds lonely in the night often hear music—there's the wind in the grass and the sheep-cries and bird-songs, and the silent music of the starry heavens—but this music was the sound of hope, and the hope was of joy. I was not sure what it said, but suddenly I knew that nothing and no one is meaningless or mean."

"I followed a star to Christmas," said one of the Wise Men. "It led me far from my own country, far from my own expectation of what Truth would be like. I found that Truth is always a revelation and a wonder, a light that no one may ever have seen before, but once seen seems to have been shining always."

Then the Child spoke: "To find what anything means, you have to look with your heart into the heart of what you're looking at. Then sometimes you see what you could not see before. I am the beautiful mystery that lies curled at the heart of all that is, waiting to be born, and my best-loved, loveliest name is love. To find me is to find Christmas."

"I think—I think I'm beginning to understand," said Ms. Darlington.

"Yes, I believe you are," said the Child. "For now we have given you all the help we can."

"There is no more?" said Ms. Darlington.

"Oh, much more!" said the Child. "But it's nothing anyone can tell you. Good-bye, Ms. Darlington, merry Christmas, and good luck!"

The crèche was once more just an ordinary crèche on the counter, waiting to be sold, and the little figures that had spoken with such animation were now just pieces of wood, not even very well carved. She stared at them for a long time. Can I possibly . . . ? she thought. She would have liked to pick up one of the figures and examine it closely, but somehow she was afraid to do that.

She slowly turned away.

She did not know how or why she turned in that direction, but suddenly right in front of her was the big natural-looking doll with which the whole affair had started, and right in front of the doll was the little girl with the thin pale face and the big brown eyes.

Ms. Darlington started to say, "I thought I told you to go home," but stopped before she said it.

"I—I just had to see her once more," said the little girl. "I—I didn't touch her."

Ms. Darlington looked at the little girl. She looked at the doll. She called a salesclerk. "I would like to buy this doll, please," she said.

When the salesclerk had written out the sales slip, Ms. Darlington took the doll and turned to the little girl.

"You bought her!" said the girl. "You must be very rich!"

"Yes, I believe I am," said Ms. Darlington, and she thrust the doll into the little girl's arms. "I bought her for you. Here, you'll need this sales slip so everyone will know she's yours."

The little girl hugged the doll to her for a moment. Then she looked up. Ms. Darlington could not tell whether the little girl was about to cry or to laugh, her eyes were welling with tears, but her face wore a look of wild joy.

"Thank you," she said, and she threw her arms around Ms. Darlington, almost crushing the doll between them. Then she turned, and holding the doll tightly in her arms, she began to run toward the escalator.

That was silly. I don't know why in the world I did that, thought Ms. Darlington.

She started down the escalator. As the moving platform trundled her gently toward the lower floor, once more she heard a voice. No, it was not a voice, but voices—the fir tree, the Santa, the little figures of the crêche, the doll, and the little girl with the pale thin face and the big brown eyes, they were all speaking as one—or was she merely hearing the carol singers the store had hired to sing? She was not sure, but somehow it did not matter.

For the voices were saying to her, "You will search for me and find me everywhere and in everything, Ms. Darlington, when you search for me with your heart."

And whatever outside herself might be celebrating or not celebrating Christmas, it was Christmas in her heart.

My Name Is Joseph

YES, MY NAME IS Joseph. I was his father, he was my son.

I see some of you smiling. But what would you have had our relation to be?

Does it disturb you to hear that when he was a boy he called me papa? As to his being the Son of God, would an old carpenter like me be the one to decide such a fine point of theology?

Oh, make no mistake, this old carpenter is not an old fool. Could I have had such a son, lived beside him all these years, and not have given much thought to many things? Do you think he would have been such a man if he'd a dolt for a father? Where do you think he got his ideas? Do you think we never talked?

But not about theology. No! That takes a more fanciful mind than mine.

As to his being the Son of God, did he claim to be? In some special way, that is, beyond the rest of you? I recall him saying, "You are all sons of God, and children of the Most High."

Whatever he was, his enemies can be satisfied now that they've finished him, haven't they? Or have they? And his friends—you are his friends, no?—you have your faith, don't you? What can I add to it?

Ah, yes, you want to ask me some questions. About what? His birth? You have heard rumors? From whom? The gossip mongers in the village? That Mary was with child before we were married? If she was, would that make her different from many other women in the village?

I know. Those among you who didn't believe he was the Messiah want me to say he was my son; to your mind that will prove he was not God's. And those who believed in him are hoping I'll say he was not my child; at least that will leave the matter open to question.

Before I say more, let me say again, I was his father, he was my son, in every way that has meaning. I held him in my arms, rocked him to sleep, tended him in his childhood illnesses, comforted him when he was hurt, embraced him when he needed embracing, chastised him when he needed that. I shared his thoughts, fears, and hopes. I saw to his schooling, taught him a trade, and made a home for him. Yes, in all that counts, we were father and son. I loved him. I believe he loved me.

Now as to his birth. Yes, it is an unusual story. Let me tell you how it occurred as nearly as I can remember after all these years.

I will begin with Mary.

When was the first time I saw Mary? When is the first time you see a lily in a field of lilies or a rose in a rose garden? She was born in my village. We were cousins. Oh, distant ones, but cousins, as were half the people there. She was a little girl among all the little girls I saw every day. When did I not see her?

But I became aware of her, not as just someone in the village, but as someone in my life, one day as I was working on a house.

A dove with a crippled wing came fluttering down the street, and after it was a gang of yelling boys trying to pelt it with stones. I suppose the dove had been intended as a sacrifice, but had gotten away. I watched for a moment. The boys weren't very accurate with their throws. But at last one stone clipped the dove, and it gave out a pitiful squawk.

At that moment, this young girl appeared. She ran between the bird and the boys, reached down, and gathered up the dove. It didn't try to avoid her. It was almost as if it knew, this was not an enemy, but a friend.

The boys came storming up and surrounded her. A torrent of words poured out of them; mostly threats and imprecations.

But the little girl stood firm, the dove clasped securely in her arms.

The tallest boy stepped forward. I knew him. His father Yousuf was a bricklayer. "That dove is ours," he said. "We found him, we chased him here. Hand him over."

The little girl said, "This dove is not yours. It is consecrated to God, and you shall not have it." The tall boy raised his hand as if to strike the girl. She didn't flinch.

I stepped forward. "Out of here, you ruffians," I cried, brandishing the hammer I happened to have in my hand. The boys disappeared.

"Thank you; oh, thank you," said the girl.

"You were brave to stand up to all those boys," I said, "but you saved your dove."

The little girl smiled. "Oh, the dove isn't mine, but it wasn't theirs either. It's God's, and they meant to harm it while I meant to bless it. God is always on the side of the gentle and kind."

I'm not so sure of that, I thought, but I said, " He was this time."

I looked at this brave and gentle little girl who was smiling gratefully up at me.

"Don't I know you? Aren't you Joachim's daughter?"

"Yes, I am," she said. "My name is Mary."

"My name is Joseph. I know your father, and your mother Anna, too. How old are you, Mary?"

"I'm ten," she said.

As I told you, I suppose I had seen this little girl almost daily for eight or nine years. I knew her parents well. But I had never looked at her before. Now I looked.

Oh, I don't mean I instantly thought I was in love with her or that she was to be my wife. After all, she was ten, I was twenty-six. But there's no doubt, I felt a deep sense of being drawn to her.

Probably all I thought was, What a pretty little girl! Or, What a brave little girl! Or, What a kind little girl! But can it be that we are drawn to one another by forces in our souls, forces we're not aware of, that make us one beyond anything we know? As she walked away, the dove cooing in her arms, I stood for a long time gazing after her.

The next day when I saw her father, he said that Mary had told him all about it, and he invited me to dinner. I was not surprised to find myself accepting.

After that, how often I found myself with them. It was only natural, I suppose. Only three months before, I had lost my wife in childbirth, and I was lonely.

Joachim's house was a religious house. There was much reading from the Torah and the prophets, strict observance of the holy days, and many prayers, usually long ones.

I'm not too religious myself, but I don't mind if others are. Joachim told me he and Anna had found themselves growing old without children. They had made a deep vow that if God should give them one, they would dedicate themselves and the child to Him. So when Mary came, they felt she was a gift from God.

I believe she felt that, too. She was not an ordinary girl. She didn't often play with other children. A girl of dreams and visions, she preferred playing by herself.

Once she told me how she felt about God. He was not something strange and mysterious and frightening, a mighty king on a far-off throne. He was a presence, warm and near. "If you will talk to Him, I'm sure He will hear you," she told me once. "I talk to Him all the time."

"What do you say to Him?" I asked.

"Oh, I just tell Him I love Him and I hope He will love me and use me in the way He will."

You might imagine talk like that would have frightened me away, but it didn't. I'm a rough carpenter, but I am also a man of deep feelings and sudden yearnings. I enjoyed being with these dear, decent people.

Often in the evening, Anna would play the lute, and we'd all join in singing religious songs. Mary was the best singer among us. There's a bird—I have never seen it and don't know what kind it is—but sometimes, working in the fields or walking through the hills, I have heard it burst into song, and I have thought if Mary were a bird, she would sound like that.

Sometimes when her mother played, Mary would dance. I liked to see her dance—she was like a field of wheat when the wind is blowing through it.

When did I cease to think of her as a girl and begin to think of her as a woman? When does a girl become a woman? At twelve, at thirteen? I don't know. But I came to realize that Mary was reaching an age when Joachim would be seeking a husband for her.

Perhaps it was one afternoon when I came upon her as she was drawing water from the well. Across the square three young men were watching her. They were talking and laughing among themselves. I couldn't hear what they were saying, but I saw how they were looking at her, and I heard them laugh. I am a man, and I know what goes through young men's minds.

Suddenly, I saw the little girl with the dove in her arms and the pack of rough boys reaching to tear it away from her! I stepped out into the square. "Mary," I called.

She waved.

I turned to the boys. "Be off," I said.

They stared at me insolently.

"Be off," I said again, and I raised my arm. My trade hasn't made me a weakling. With another insolent look, off they went.

It was then, I suppose, as I walked Mary home, I realized that in a short time she must be promised to someone. The thought that the someone might be someone other than myself was an unthinkable thought. I was in love with Mary! I believe the realization that I was in love with her came as a surprise.

Looking back now, I think I always had been in love with her, from that first moment when I saw the little girl with the dove. From that moment she was my dove.

I was twice her age, but I didn't think that was important. I was still a young man. I was healthy and strong. I was of good stock. I could trace my lineage to David the King. I wasn't rich, but I was as rich as Joachim. I had a reputation as a craftsman and I earned enough to keep a family comfortable.

Above all, I loved her. And while I didn't know that she loved me—I had never allowed myself to think in such terms before—at least I knew she thought of me as her friend, and it's no long leap from friendship to love.

So I sought out Joachim and Anna and proposed to them that Mary and I should be betrothed to be married.

Much to my delight, they were more than willing. Joachim laughed. "This comes as no surprise," he said. "Anna and I have wondered for a long time when you were going to speak for her. We have both said many times, 'He loves the girl. What is he waiting for?' I assure you there is no one to whom we would rather see our daughter married."

"Thank you, thank you, my friend," I said. "I love Mary. Do you think she loves me?"

"Can there be a doubt?" said Joachim. "She has even told us how much she likes you."

"Like and love, they are not the same," I said. "I like you, but I'm not in love with you. I want to be Mary's husband; I want her to be my wife."

"Mary is an obedient daughter," said Joachim. "She will do as I say."

"I don't want her to do as you say," I said. "I want her to do as she wishes."

"I don't know if she loves you or not," said Anna. "I don't know if she's ever thought of you like that. I doubt if she's ever thought of anyone like that. I didn't love Joachim when I was betrothed to him, I hardly knew him. I had only met him once. But I learned to love him."

"We've had a good marriage," said Joachim.

"You marry and you learn to love one another," said Anna. "You're a good man, Joseph. Mary will learn to love you."

"I'm not very good-looking," I said, doubtfully.

"Is Joachim good-looking?" said Anna, laughing. Joachim snorted.

"Like Joachim," Anna went on, "you are more than good-looking. You're kind. You're gentle. You're strong. And you are already dear to her."

"I wouldn't want her to be my wife if she didn't want to be," I said.

"I will ask her," said Joachim.

"No, if she thinks you want her to marry me, she will say yes."

"Then ask her yourself. Here, I'll call her in."

When we were alone, I didn't know what to say; I didn't know what to do. I just stood and looked at her.

"Yes, Joseph?" she said.

"Mary," I said at last.

"Yes, Joseph?"

"Mary, I have something to say to you."

"Yes, Joseph?"

"I have spoken to your father and mother."

"Yes, Joseph!"

"I have asked that we might be betrothed!"

For a moment I thought I caught a flicker of—was it fear?—in her eyes. Then her face composed itself.

"And what did they say, Joseph?"

"They said they were willing."

"I, too, am willing," she said. Then she smiled. She has an extraordinary smile, a woman's smile. She was smiling—why should I be anything but smiling, too? A great wave of happiness bounded through my heart.

I took her hands in mine. "Mary, I love you," I said.

Again she smiled. "Joseph, dear Joseph."

"This is not a sudden thing," I said. "I've loved you ever since the day I first saw you—the day with the dove."

"I'm glad for that day, too," she said.

"I love you as a husband loves his wife," I said. "Can you love me as a wife loves her husband?"

"I will love you in whatever way God decrees I should love you," she said. "If I'm to be your wife, I will love you as a wife."

"Do you know what it means for me to be your husband and for you to be my wife?"

"Of course, I do," she said with a smile. "It means that we shall live together and I will be the mother of your children."

I wondered if she knew what the words she was saying meant. There was about Mary—as there still is—a veil of innocence. Some people are innocents, no matter what befalls them. I've always felt in Mary—is this why I've loved her so?—an unstained and unstainable essence, the eternal virgin that perhaps every woman in her secret heart always is.

I shall remember always how we stood there, hand in hand and heart in heart, and I clasped to me a vision of innocence—pure, virginal, perfect—that I have never let go.

So the betrothal took place. We pledged ourselves to one another. I was a very happy man. If I had frequented Joachim's house before, now I haunted it. A year is a long time to wait. A month passed, another month, several months.

Then the impossible occurred. I believe it was a Sabbath—as was their custom, they had invited me to eat with them—when Mary told me her story. Her incredible story about an angel coming to her and telling her she was to have a child by the Most High! You all must have heard some form of it—that's why you're asking for my version, isn't it?

Naturally the story astounded me. Oh, I know what you're thinking, I must have been outraged. No, not at first. The thought that Mary might be deceiving me hardly passed through my mind.

When she told me her story, it was so incredible it never occurred to me it was anything but a young girl's fantasy. She has had a crazy dream, I thought. How can she possibly know she is with child? To be sure of that takes—what—three months?

"How can you know?" I asked.

"The angel told me," she said. "And I just know."

That's a woman's thinking, I thought.

The visit of the angel and even his words to her—this she had clearly. But when I pressed her for details as to what had happened after that, she couldn't tell me.

"The Most High came to you?" I would ask.

"I—I don't know," she'd say. "I think so."

"Did something happen?"

She would look at me strangely and nod her head.

"What?" I would ask, but when I pressed her, she would only shake her head.

"I can't—I can't—" she would say. Her eyes would fill with confusion, but at the same time I could see they were full of a radiance as

if she were remembering an experience beyond her power to put into words.

"You saw something?"

"No."

"You heard something?"

"No."

"You experienced something?"

Again that strange look, half confusion, half ecstasy, would shine in her eyes.

I asked her many times. I have asked her many times since then—that's only natural, isn't it, considering what's happened since?—and I've never had more of an answer than she gave me then.

You must decide for yourself what you will believe. Just as I had to decide. For I did have to decide.

The three months passed, and then there was no longer any doubt. Mary was with child.

Before that I'd had to wonder about a fantasy. Now I had to wrestle with a fact. The woman I loved was with child and I had never touched her! Could it be, could it possibly be that this lovely one that I loved had deceived me? Oh, the sleepless nights of deep and agonizing doubts that followed then!

You can understand how I felt. I was angry. I was humiliated. I was tortured. Mary was a very pretty young woman—she is still beautiful—and in the village there were many handsome young men, not twice her age like me.

I thought, I shall drag her before the priest and make her drink the bitter water mixed with dirt from the floor of the tabernacle and watch her rot with it. I shall make her a public shame as she has made me a private anguish.

But that Mary was unfaithful to me was impossible for me to believe for long. Yes, even more impossible than the story she was telling.

I was certain Mary loved me. I had not been deluding myself all these months. I felt I knew this woman as well as I knew myself. She loved me!

Moreover, I felt it would be impossible for her to lie; she wouldn't even know how to lie. Most of us are capable of deceit. But I have known one or two persons who had no seeds of deceit in them. Mary is one of these.

What advantage could she hope to gain by telling such a farfetched story? It only made anyone who might doubt her doubt her even more.

The longer I thought about it, the less I found myself doubting, the more I found myself wondering. Oh, I say it calmly now. I didn't come to it calmly. I agonized to it.

I am a practical man. All my life I've worked with hammer and saw, wood and nails, with real things in a real world. But was what she said had happened impossible? I knew that many people believe in Messiahs. Very well, couldn't I? And if one should come, might this not be the way he would choose? Wasn't Moses found among the bulrushes? Wasn't David a shepherd's son? Marvelous things do happen. And if such a thing could happen, would not Mary be such a one as it might happen to? Mary is and always was as religious as I am not. I'll admit I've sometimes thought the right word is superstitious. She believes easily. It's as easy for her to believe as it is hard for me.

I know a lot of you believe in angels and the like—I think that's why you see them. I've never had much faith in them myself.

But if there aren't angels and you imagine them, wouldn't it follow that if there were angels you would be the ones to see them?

You can see how I argued with myself. I became my own angels' advocate. By this time I was beginning to see them myself. I don't believe in dreams, but I found myself waking from dreams where I was talking to angels. They were telling me to believe what she was saying. You can understand that, can't you? Dear God, I wanted to!

Once I began to hope it could be possible, I began to think of reasons why it might be. Had her parents not pledged her to God? Had not she herself all her life prayed to Him to use her? And if she was to be used by the Most High, was there a better way that He might use her? To have a child—was that not a natural function for a woman? And if there were ever an unsullied vessel for the Lord to express Himself through, wasn't it this innocent woman who was to be my wife?

When you're faced with something like this, it's a very confused and confusing moment in your life. There was my personal unbelief, but there was my wish to believe. There was my practical knowledge of the world, but there was my deep trust in Mary's honesty. There was my hurt pride—and there was my love.

Yes, there was my love. In the end there's no doubt as to what made me decide as I decided. I loved her. I loved her in a real and practical way—like the carpenter I was who wanted a wife to make him a home and give him children. But I loved her, too, in a beautiful and ideal way—like the young man in love I also was, who wanted an impossible and unsullied vision of perfection he could hold in his mind and dream about. For four years I'd had such a vision. Could I abandon it now? Could I give her up without giving myself up? Without her, would life be life? Or would it be merely an empty passage from empty day to empty night?

Mary felt she had been chosen by something beyond herself. I, too, had no choice. I was driven by my deepest needs and by my highest vision of what life must be to be worth living.

Whatever had happened, whatever would happen, Mary was my wife, Mary was my life. If I had to choose between believing I had been deceived or believing in a wonder, than I chose the wonder.

But before the child was delivered, another extraordinary event occurred. The Romans ordered a census. Every man had to return to the town he had been born in. I had to go to Bethlehem.

Mary didn't have to go with me—the Romans weren't interested in counting women in their census—and I thought she should stay with her mother. It is a four-day trip to Bethlehem, and I knew the baby might be coming any day.

But she insisted on going. "Everything will be all right," she said. "You can take care of me."

I'm not sure of that, I thought. Still, I was pleased that she wanted to be with me. And I decided it might be just as well if the baby were born somewhere else. You know how such things are. The townspeople didn't know anything for sure. But every town has a few gossipers. Some of them had heard tales about an angel; I think there was some snickering—behind our backs, of course.

So I thought if the baby came into the world in some part of it where no one knew us, it might be better for him and for us.

It was late afternoon when we came down the hill into Bethlehem. The trip hadn't been hard—we had a donkey and Mary rode most of the way—and the road had run through pretty country.

There was an inn at the edge of town. In the courtyard, as I helped Mary down, suddenly she gasped and said to me, "Joseph, you'll have to find a place for us quickly. The baby will be here tonight."

The inn was crowded, dirty, noisy. I saw some men who sounded drunk and some women who didn't look any better than they might be. I went in search of the innkeeper.

When I told him I wanted a room, he laughed at me. "There isn't a room to be had in Bethlehem tonight."

"My wife is about to have a baby."

"If she was about to have a menagerie of babies, I couldn't help you," he said. "I've got people sleeping out in the courtyard. Sorry."

"She can't have the baby in the street," I said.

He started to turn away, but something in my face and voice must have made him turn back. "Have the pains begun?" he said.

I nodded. "I think so."

"You think so? Is this your first baby?"

I nodded.

"Look. Back on the hillside about half a mile, you'll find some stables. I keep my goats there. You'll probably find a cow or two and a few sheep. But if you're not too proud, it will be a shelter from the weather and you can find some clean straw to lie in."

"Thank you, thank you," I said. "You're sure it's all right?"

"Of course, I'm sure. You go on up there and later this evening I'll have my wife look in on you. She's had six children and helped the neighbors with another dozen," he said.

We found the stable as he said we would—a cave in the hillside. There were a few animals, but they didn't mind us, so we didn't mind them.

I made Mary a bed in the straw, and about midnight the baby was born. It was a boy, as she had said it would be.

The innkeeper's wife didn't get there until after the baby was born, though I was glad for her help when she came. So I had to take charge of the birth myself. There were just the two of us. Mary and me. Mary was hardly more than a child herself. And I was scared. Oh, I was scared. Remember, I had lost a wife in childbirth once. I had never realized how much a woman has to give to give birth. I wiped the sweat from her face. I held her hand when she cried out. I wish there had been somebody there to hold mine.

So it was that I helped him into the world. I tied off the cord. I heard his first cry. I saw his first breath. I gave him to his mother and watched her as she wrapped him in swaddling cloths. I got some clean straw and made a bed for him in a manger. There was nothing supernatural about his coming into the world, if that's what you're expecting. He was born just like every other baby is born.

Mary kept telling me she wanted to hold the baby and I kept telling her she should rest. But after a while I laid him in her arms.

"He's my beautiful son," she said. Then she looked at me and smiled. "Our son!" For a long time I sat beside her in the straw, my arm around her to support her and draw her close.

Some of you have sons, and you know what it's like to have your first. Now that I've had several sons and daughters, I can take them more as a matter of course. But that first one, ah, that was something! Yes, mine or God's! They are all God's, aren't they?

He was a handsome handful of a boy. "He looks like you," I told her. "He has your eyes." Mary's eyes have always been deep dark pools. I have always thought she has the most beautiful eyes I've ever seen, but then I've always thought she was the most beautiful woman I've ever seen.

"I think he looks amazingly like you," she said.

I looked at him closely and I really couldn't see much resemblance, but I hoped it would turn out that way. And I believe it did, don't you? He did come to look amazingly like me. But the truth is, a newborn baby looks like nothing but a newborn baby.

The baby was only a few hours old when the shepherds came in—there were two of them—and poured out their tale—you've all heard it, I know, so I won't tell it again—how angels had appeared to them as they were keeping their sheep and told them a baby had been born in Bethlehem who was to be the Messiah. Their story was a garbled one, but they were excited and both trying to speak at the same time.

I tried to argue with them that maybe someone else in the city had had a baby, someone of importance. But they said, "No, the voice told us we would find him in a manger wrapped in swaddling cloths."

In a few days those shepherds had carried their story—they'd straightened out the details between them—all over Bethlehem, and after that all kinds of people came to see us.

We named the baby Jeshua; Mary chose the name.

Most of those who came to see us were just curious, I think. But many of them brought us food and gifts, and I was thankful for everything anyone did. I was especially interested in three of them who came together. One of the shepherds told me he had heard they were kings. They spoke with an accent. They were obviously rich, for they gave us some very rich gifts. They told me they were Persians and priests in their own country. They said their own prophet—he had lived a thousand years before—I think his name was Zarathustra—had foretold that a Messiah was coming. And this is the interesting thing: he had said that the Messiah was to be born of a virgin. When I heard that, I told them Mary's story.

"We were certain that was how it was," they said. "We had seen the signs in the heavens. A star led us to this place before we knew where you were."

These men made a great impression on me. They were powerful, rich, learned, and I could see they believed the whole story about the angels and that the boy was the son of the Most High. Still, they were foreigners—and I think foreigners have all kinds of superstitious beliefs—and also they were priests—and I think priests are likely to believe anything.

I just wish that once somebody like myself, an everyday kind of man, had come and told me he had seen angels or followed a star or heard a voice. One of the things that struck me—from beginning to end, it was always the people one might expect to have these visions who had them; it never was merchants or accountants or carpenters.

No, it was these foreign priests given to looking for mysterious signs in the heavens. Or simple fellows like those shepherds, with a lifetime of lonely nights spent out on the hills with nothing but sheep and stars and wind—I imagine visions and voices come easily there. Or an only child like Mary, who lived in her own imagination, drenched from her birth with religious notions. Sometimes I wish I were like them.

Oh, I came to believe. Yes, I think I did. But always there were the doubts. Nothing ever happened, as far as I personally was concerned, that could not be naturally explained. I'm just not religious enough, I guess.

In fact, here comes the only real reason to believe I ever had. Here comes my wife. As you know, *she* thinks he was the Messiah.

I suppose it ought to make me proud to think that maybe he was. But that's not what makes me proud. I'm proud of him as my son, proud that he had the courage to be what he was, even if I didn't always understand him.

Those angels are supposed to have said he was to bring peace and goodwill to all the earth, and he hasn't done that—there are about as many people fighting and warring as always—but he did set a lot of people thinking, didn't he? He taught them they had to love one another, and that's the way to peace.

He spoke out for what he believed was true, and he did what he thought was right, and he got killed for it, but what he lived for didn't die. No, or you wouldn't be here asking me all these questions.

Maybe you ought to talk to Mary, too. She'll give you a lot of different answers than I have. She was with him to the end. I didn't go with him myself. But the way things turned out, I think I did him as much good staying home as I would have by going with him. He knew I loved him. He had his work to do and I had mine. Maybe if there weren't people like him living as he lived and teaching what he taught, the world wouldn't be worth living in. But if there were no one like me sawing and hammering and nailing things together, the world would have fallen down around our heads long ago. . . .

Mary dearest, can you come over here? These people would like to talk with you . . . about our son.

Imagination, Imagination!

THE BOY CAME UP the street, swinging a small white bag. The bag contained the gifts he had gotten at the Mayor's Christmas Tree Party—ten little Indians and some hard candy. He had taken out and examined the Indians as soon as he had gotten them. They seemed like good Indians to him. He was eating a piece of the candy as he walked. Occasionally he kicked at clumps of sooty snow, all that remained from a snowfall two days before.

As he crossed the viaduct, a freight train came snailing underneath. So he climbed onto the railing, hooked his legs between the balustrades, and leaned as far out over the tracks as he could.

The train enmeshed all his senses—sight, sound, feeling, smell, even taste—perhaps taste most of all, for he tasted it with all of him. The huge, lumbering cars came squirting out directly underneath him. Their thunder enveloped him. It shook the railing he was perched on. He could feel it in his bones.

He counted the cars as they came. A block ahead, the track curved. There he could see the names of the railroads printed on the sides of the cars. He tried to count the cars in his head and at the same time speak the names out loud. He had caught the name and number of the locomotive before it disappeared around the curve. It was number 1429 of the Atchison, Topeka, and Santa Fe. But the cars were from everywhere, Wabash, Union Pacific, Illinois Central, Gulf, Milwaukee Road, Erie Lackawanna, Missouri Kansas Texas, Seaboard Coast Line, Cotton Belt, Canadian Pacific, Frisco, Chesapeake & Ohio, Burlington Northern, Grand Trunk Western. He hadn't known there were that many! How did they all get in one train?

He wished he could be on that train. He'd like to slip down off this old viaduct, run out across the tracks, reach up, and clamber onto one of those cars. Be a hobo. He'd read about hobos. That was the good life! No one to tell you anything. No one to ask you anything. If you could just outwit the railroad police!

Yep, he'd come down here one day and hop one of these freights, if he could find a slow one. He'd be afraid to hop a fast one. Maybe he'd be afraid to hop a slow one. It was dangerous—he know that. He'd never been close to a train, except like this, hanging over a viaduct, and once in a station. But then it was going slow. He'd heard if you get too close to the wheels when they are turning fast, they just draw you under. He bet that was true.

Sitting up here, watching the cars come sliding out, surrounded by their thunder, he could feel their fascinating pull.

An automobile came by on the street and as it passed him, honked. The sound made him jerk upright, and as he did, his bag of Indians and candy caught on the concrete rail and tore out of his hand. He clutched at it wildly, but it fell onto one of the freight cars passing underneath, and went gliding off down the tracks.

As the car made the curve, he read its name—Denver & Rio Grande Western.

He wondered where his bag would go. Denver & Rio Grande Western! It sounded like adventure, cowboys, Mexicans, mountains, rivers. He wondered if some hobo would find his bag. If he did, he bet he'd like the candy. He didn't know if a hobo would want the Indians.

He hated to lose those Indians! He was sure glad he had eaten some of the candy.

He went slowly up the street toward the house where he lived. It was not his house. He had a room in it. His mother and stepfather had two rooms, a kitchen and a bedroom, across the hall. He went into his room. There was no one there. He hadn't expected anybody to be there. He looked in the closet, then under the bed. You never know, there might be somebody lurking to pounce on him. Then he went into his mother's rooms. There was no one there either. He hadn't expected there would be. His mother, he knew, was working. His stepfather was probably working, too, unless he had the day off—then he would be in a bar somewhere.

In the kitchen he took a slice of bread out of the refrigerator, smeared it with peanut butter, and ate it at the kitchen table.

They had lived in these rooms only three days. He had to admit they were an improvement over where they had lived before—the St. James Hotel, what a dump! Nobody lived there except old folks like his mother and stepfather. That's where they had lived ever since his mother had brought him away from home to Kansas City and he'd found he had a stepfather. He hated to think about that.

At first he had thought it might be fun to be in Kansas City. There would be cowboys and Indians. But after three months he hadn't seen any. Kansas City was just like Wilmington, only bigger—and there weren't any friends. Anyway, there might as well not be any. He had made a couple of friends—yes, pretty good friends—in school. But today they were home with their families celebrating Christmas. That's where everybody was—except him.

He wasn't celebrating Christmas, there wasn't any Christmas to celebrate. Here he was all alone in a dingy rooming house a thousand miles away from everybody he knew, except his mother and step-father. And he might as well be a thousand miles away from them.

He hadn't gotten anything for Christmas, except those Indians and candy, and he had lost them. Oh, his mother had promised she would get him some Christmas gifts as soon as she could, but what with their moving and all that—there were all kinds of problems, she said—she just hadn't had time to get them. But he would get them, she said he would get them. But what kind of Christmas gifts would be Christmas gifts when they weren't on Christmas!

He had been feeling sorry for himself all day. Now he began to feel sorrier. He felt as if he were going to blubber, and he didn't want to blubber. There was nobody to hear him. So he let out a string of oaths. Cursing helped him not to cry.

He got out another piece of bread and smeared it with peanut butter and jelly and ate that. As he ate, he noticed a candle on a shelf by the sink. He hadn't seen it before. It was a Santa Claus candle, red coat, red cap, white beard.

He felt a flare of anger—against his mother, against Santa Claus, against the world. There isn't any Santa Claus, he thought. He's nothing but this lousy candle, or a guy with a fake beard in a department store.

He picked up the candle. It grinned at him. He carried it into his own room and set it on his chest of drawers. He wished he hadn't lost his Indians. They could have tied Santa to the stake and set fire to him. That's what he deserved.

He thought about those Indians. He wondered where they'd be by now, trailing out over Kansas, heading west, he felt sure. Lucky Indians! He wished he were with them. He picked up the Santa Claus again. Maybe he ought to set fire to him anyway, he didn't need those Indians. He went to the closet and got out a cardboard box. He sat down on the floor and turned the box upside down in front of him. Out spilled a clutter of marbles and bottle caps. He carefully separated the marbles by color. Then he separated the bottle caps by brand. They were mostly Coca-Cola, but he had a lot of soda-pop tops, grape, cream, strawberry, orange, and several caps from beer bottles. He turned the bottle caps upside down. Then they slid easily. This enabled him to play all kinds of games. He could slide them against one another. When they struck, if one turned over, he was dead, or at least out of the game. That way he could fight duels, joust, stage battles. The marbles usually became cavalry—or artillery. By shooting them back and forth between the bottle caps, he could fight gun battles.

He went back into his mother's bedroom. He got a shaving brush that his stepfather had, and a small bottle of his mother's perfume, one of those thin bottles with a fancy gold top. It looked like his mother, smelled like her, too. He put these up on top of his chest with the Santa Claus. Then he lined up his marbles and bottle caps in neat rows on the rug and they became men—soldiers, cowboys, pirates, knights. Out of their midst, he moved a small aggie—his favorite marble—and the aggie became himself.

"I have called you here to announce the dire news of a national disaster," said the aggie that had become a boy—or was it the boy who had become an aggie? "As you know, there has been no Christmas this year." A murmur of dismay rose from the bottle cap ranks. "I have now found out the reason. The giants have kidnapped Santa Claus."

A dreadful groan went up. "The beautiful giantess—you all know how pretty she looks and how good she smells"—he pointed to the perfume bottle—"and how evil she is at heart—and old bristle brush, the cruel giant—I don't have to tell any of you how wicked he is—he has torn many of you bottle caps away from your beer bottle homes—these two have captured Santa Claus and taken him to their castle on top of the Impossible Mountain. They have issued a decree. There will be no more Christmas."

Again, a groan sounded from the multitude assembled on the rug, which had now become a city square.

The rug was capable of being anything. It was woven in an intricate pattern, every feature of which could be anything the boy wanted it to be—a city, a castle, a street, a road, a field, a forest, a stream, a lake, a hedgerow. The rug could be as big as China or as small as a single building.

"Do you think we can rescue him?"

"I don't see how we can. We can't get up Impossible Mountain," said one of the bottle caps; he was a cream soda bottle cap. When he played knights, the boy usually made this bottle cap Prince John, Richard the Lionhearted's cowardly brother. The boy had only contempt for him. He was always among the first to give up. In a siege, he advised surrender, and in a battle he was quick to break and run.

For a moment the boy was unsure what he should do. Then he picked up another of his marbles. This was a steelie. Usually he did not like the steelie. All the other marbles being glass, the steelie always felt as if it could smash its way through them like an arrogant bully.

But now the steelie had become a young man with long red-gold hair, cold gray steely eyes, and iron-strong muscles. He was clad in a bear skin and thonged sandals. On his right hand he wore an iron glove, and in it he twirled, as lightly as an Indian club, a gigantic hammer.

"If there's giants around, I'd like to be in on this," said the young man in a voice that boomed like thunder.

"Hail, Thor," said the boy, "god of thunder."

Thor raised his hammer in imperial salute.

"It's giants all right," said the boy. "And the worst kind. It's—" the boy paused—"it's Sorry, the beautiful giantess" (his mother's name was Sarah) "she's really more a witch than a giantess."

"I've heard of Sorry," said Thor. "She's the most dangerous kind. She looks pretty and good, but deep down underneath, she's terrible."

"And the giant is Bung," said the boy. (His stepfather's name was Ben.)

"I know that Bung," said Thor, twirling his hammer even more menacingly. "And I know nothing I'd like better than to get him in hammer range."

With a mighty heave he cast his hammer from him. The hammer flew through the air with a rumble and a flash and then flew back into his hand.

"How far will it fly?" said the boy.

"A hundred miles," said Thor, carefully wiping the blade of the hammer with his hand. "Got to keep it clean, you know. Sometimes it accidentally hits a troll or a goblin. Troll dust wrecks my aim."

The boy nodded sagely. "I'm sure glad you could come. You're my favorite god, you know."

"Always glad to help a friend," said Thor, "especially where there's giants. I hate giants."

"I know," said the boy. "Thor, the giant killer! When I first read about you, I got a hammer just like Mjolner and hid it under my bed."

"Kill any giants?"

"No, but I kept it just in case."

"Good boy!" said Thor. "Just what wicked deeds have these giants done?"

"They've kidnapped Santa Claus," said the boy.

"Kidnapped Santa Claus? There won't be any Christmas."

"There hasn't been," said the boy, looking around the bare room. "You can see that. No tree."

Thor said, "Faugh!"

"No presents."

"Faugh!"

"No nothing!"

"Giants!" snarled Thor. "If they had their way, there wouldn't ever be anything worth having. I've heard them talking when they didn't know I was listening. You ought to hear what they think about birthdays and even fireworks on Fourth of July. What have these dirty giants done with Santa Claus?"

"They're holding him on top of Impossible Mountain."

Thor whistled. "That's a magic mountain."

"Do you think we ought to get more help?" said the boy.

"From these?" said Thor, waving his hand contemptuously over the bottle caps and marbles. "Faugh!"

"Let's give them one more chance," said the boy. "Would any of you brave men want to go with us to rescue Santa Claus from the giants?"

None moved.

"Just as I thought," said Thor. "Sniveling cowards, afraid of the giants!"

"Oh well," said the boy, "there's two giants, there's two of us. Two against two, that's fair."

The two started toward the mountain. It was a long way to the mountain, and not an easy one. The chest of drawers stood at the edge of the rug, and the rug was now a wild country, hundreds of miles wide, uninhabited and trackless. The aggie and the steelie had to push their way through thick forests, around hedgerows, and over lakes and streams.

There were adventures every foot of the way. They had to get around Fafnir, the famous dragon—he was a sock. After him, there was a band of Moors—all his brown marbles, about twenty of them—who came charging out of ambush. They had hardly beaten off the Moors when up rode the Black Knight of the Glen. He was a black marble with one white stripe, and the boy knew him for a villain. Thor offered to knock out his brains with his hammer, but the boy said, no, the rules of chivalry required that he should engage him hand to hand, and the two fought a long and chancy battle before the boy gave him the coup de grace.

So it went all afternoon. Even when they drew near the Impossible Mountain and could see it looming above them, six Zulus—bottle caps—came shrieking toward them casting their assegais—toothpicks.

At last the two adventurers came out into a wide plain (the bare floor beyond the rug) and stared up at Impossible Mountain.

"These must be mountain giants," said Thor. "There are two kinds, you know. Mountain and frost."

"The man may be a mountain giant, but the giantess is frost. She has a heart of ice," said the boy. He had a sudden inspiration. He ran to the kitchen and got a large glass bowl. This he placed over the shaving brush, perfume bottle, and Santa candle. Then he turned to Thor. "They live in an ice palace on top of the mountain. And what those giants would like is to turn Santa's heart to ice like their own."

"We'd better be quick then," said Thor. "How are we going to get up the mountain?"

"I have a friend who lives near here," said the boy. "Maybe he can help us."

The boy found a small cardboard box and set it down by one leg of the chest. In the box he placed a green bottle cap, and he rolled the aggie in front of it.

"Are you home, Jack?" he called.

"Who's there?" said Jack—for the green bottle cap was now Jack—coming out of the box.

"It's me," said the boy. The two whispered together for a few minutes.

Then the boy turned to Thor. "This is my friend Jack. He says he's glad to help us up the mountain."

"Why, he's just a boy," said Thor.

The boy thought, Being a boy is not so bad, and he started to say, He can get us up the mountain. That's more than you can do, Thor, but he held his tongue. And all he said was, "He's a giant-killer like you."

"The god with the hammer!" said Thor. "And my hammer wants to meet your head."

There was a longer moment of silence.

Then they heard the giant talking to the giantess. "This fellow Thor is a bully. And mean. Real mean. He's a killer."

"Yeah, a giant killer!" shouted Thor.

"Maybe we ought to send for help," said the giantess.

"I think they're scared of us!" said the boy.

"They're scared of me!" said Thor.

The boy wished he hadn't picked that steelie to be Thor. The steelie was obnoxious, no matter what he picked him to be, and Thor was getting to be more obnoxious by the moment.

"What do you want?" cried the giant.

The boy shouted, "We want you to let Santa Claus go so people can have Christmas."

"That's what *he* wants," cried Thor. "I want to bust your heads."

The boy turned toward Thor angrily. "Don't you ever think of anything except busting people's heads?"

"Just giants' heads."

"Giants are people," cried the giantess.

"Faugh!" said Thor. He turned to the boy. "What are we wasting time for? My hammer will smack right through that ice palace and shatter it to bits."

"But if you do that," said the boy, "sharp icicles will fly everywhere. They might kill Santa Claus."

"So what? It would kill those giants," said Thor.

"But we came to rescue Santa Claus."

"That's why you came. What's important is getting rid of giants. As for Santa Claus, isn't he an elf? Elves aren't much better than giants. I've busted a lot of elf heads in my time."

"Santa Claus is not just an elf," said the boy. "I love Santa Claus. Everybody loves him."

"You human beings!" said Thor. "You're always letting mush like love keep you from doing what needs to be done. We gods aren't like that." Thor took a firm grip on his hammer and began to draw back his arm.

The boy had had no idea when he had started out on this adventure that he would have to fight Thor as well as giants, but that is the way of adventures. They take unexpected twists and turns—that's what makes them adventures. Thor was turning out to be an unbearable bully.

The boy leaped in front of Thor, threw up his hands, and cried, "Thor, stop!"

"Get out of the way, boy."

"No!"

The boy was scared. But he was the one who had brought Thor here and it was up to him to stop Thor if he could. He knew he was no match for him; Thor was the mightiest of all the gods. But wait! Was he? Wasn't there a god mightier even than Thor?

This is Christmas Day, he thought. A song his mother had taught him came into his head. The only line he could remember was, "O little Lord Jesus, asleep in the hay," but as he sang that, he reached down among his bottle caps and chose one that was shiny silver. It was one of his favorites. He set this bottle cap on top of the chest in front of the steelie and the aggie. And the bottle cap was not a bottle cap but a baby, and the lace of the doily on which it reposed was not lace, but the straw of the manger in which the baby lay.

Thor let out a roar of astonishment and rage and let his hammer drop. "What kind of humbuggery are you trying to pull on me?" he cried.

The baby ignored Thor. He looked up at the boy and smiled. "You called for my help, I believe."

"But can you help me? You—you're just a baby."

"What did you expect the little Lord Jesus asleep in the hay to be? This is my birthday, isn't it?"

"But what can you do against a powerful guy like Thor?" said the boy.

"God, not guy!" said Thor.

"Why don't you ask Thor?" said the baby.

"Do you know this baby, Thor?"

Thor snarled an unprintable reply and muttered, "He deceives you with those baby looks."

"I'm afraid Thor doesn't care much for me," said the baby. "Do you, Thor?"

"Faugh! The world was a good world before you came into it, fit for iron men and gods." He took a menacing grip on his hammer.

"He—he's likely to bash you," said the boy.

"No, he's not likely to. He just would like to. He's tried many times. When he does, that magic hammer flies back, but not to his hand. It hits him on the head." The baby chuckled. "What you send out comes back, that's the rule."

"Your rule!" Thor sneered, but he did not try to use his hammer. At last he turned to the boy. "I thought you and I were friends."

"I am your friend," said the boy.

"Naw, you're not tough enough. You're a softie like this baby. Faugh! I hope the giants get all of you."

As he spoke, a flash of lightning and a roar of thunder filled the air. Thor had disappeared. The steelie was in the boy's pocket.

"He was right, you know. You are a lot like me," said the baby.

The boy liked that idea, that maybe he was like the little Lord Jesus. But then he said quickly, "I'm not a baby."

"Of course not. But you're not a bully either. You don't even like bullies."

"No," said the boy. That was certainly true.

"Remember your first day at school? You stopped that big boy from beating on a smaller one."

"Yeah," said the boy.

"And Thor, you showed him what you think of bullies!"

"Yeah. Yeah, I did," said the boy.

"You and I have a lot in common," said the baby. "Take Christmas. You're feeling left out, aren't you?"

"I sure am," said the boy, his lip trembling.

"You and I don't cry about being left out," said the baby sternly. "Think how I felt that first Christmas. At least you have a room. There was no room for me. All I had was a little straw and a stable."

"Yeah," said the boy.

"So what's our problem?" said the baby.

"The giants have kidnapped Santa Claus and are turning his heart to ice in their ice palace," said the boy.

"We can't have that," said the baby. "We have to get the giants to let him go."

"How about blasting them with one of your miracles?" said the boy eagerly.

The baby frowned. "You go to Sunday school, don't you?"

"Oh, sure," said the boy. Then he added, "Sometimes."

"Then you ought to know my methods. I never blast my enemies. I love them and forgive them."

"Love them and forgive them?" said the boy.
"It takes a big man to use my methods."
"I don't think it will work with giants," said the boy.
"Do you have some better idea?"
The boy shook his head. No, he didn't. When he had started out with Thor, it had looked as if saving Santa would be a lark—Thor would bash the giants and Santa would be free—but things had not turned out as expected. His thinking to call the Baby Jesus was a sudden Christmas inspiration; he was proud of that—he had to save Santa, he dared not fail, the happiness of the whole world depended on him—but how was he going to do it?
"You don't really want to blast those giants," said the baby. "You wouldn't let Thor do it."
"No," said the boy.
"You're not a blaster any more than I am. Wouldn't you really rather have love than blasting? You love me, don't you?"
"Oh, sure."
"And Santa?"
"I'll say."
"And your mother?"
The boy nodded.
"And your stepfather?"
"No," cried the boy.
"Wouldn't you like to?"
"He doesn't love me!" said the boy.
"He brought you with him, didn't he? He didn't have to. Think about it. They won't be expecting love, will they?"
"They sure won't."
"It will take them by surprise, won't it?"
There was no doubt about that, thought the boy. It had taken him by surprise. It was a surprising idea. He began to turn it over in his mind.
"Hey, it will be a surprise," he said. "Yeah, a kind of secret weapon. Hey, that's not a bad idea. Love, the secret weapon."
"I thought you'd see its possibilities," said the baby.
"Love, the secret weapon," said the boy again. "Yeah, I like that. They'll never know what hit them."
"All right, come over here," said the baby. "We're going to shower our love all over them."

The boy ran to the kitchen. He came back with a sugar bowl. He scattered a pinch of sugar over the glass bowl that was the giants' palace.

"Hey, you giants," cried the boy. "You feel that? You're being zapped by love!"

"Hey, it's snowing," said the giant seeing the white crystals sparkling down. He stuck his head out of the ice palace and the boy sprinkled a pinch of sugar on him. "Hey, this isn't snow," the giant told the giantess, "it's sweet."

The giantess stuck her head out of the ice palace and the boy sprinkled sugar on her. "It is sweet," she said. "It makes me feel good."

The giant threw down his club. "I don't know when I've felt this sweet," he said. "I feel like I want to be sweet to everybody."

"Hey, you giants," shouted the boy. "You know why you're feeling so sweet? You're being zapped with love!"

"Love? What's that?" said the giant.

"I knew you wouldn't know," said the boy. "It's our secret weapon."

"I like it," said the giant. "It makes me feel so sweet. I don't feel mean anymore."

"Then you admit you've been mean?" said the boy.

"We don't want to be," said both the giants. "We want to be sweet and good."

"You have icy hearts!" said the boy.

"We don't want icy hearts. That's why we kidnapped Santa, so he would make our hearts warm like his."

"Will you let him go?"

"Oh, sure, we don't need him anymore, now that we have love."

"Okay, here's more love," said the boy. He sprinkled another pinch of sugar onto them.

"Thank you, thank you," cried the giants.

"Now aren't you sorry for all the mean things you've done?" said the boy.

"Yes, yes," cried the giants, falling on their knees. "Please forgive us."

"You'll be better in the future?"

"Yes, yes, we promise."

"And never kidnap Santa again?"

"Never, never."
"Cross your hearts?"
"Cross our hearts!" The giants began to cry.
"Good!" said the boy. "Good!" With the giants on their knees crying, a warm feeling of deep satisfaction began to pour through him. He sprinkled another pinch of sugar on them. "You're forgiven," he said—then he remembered something from Sunday school—"Go and sin no more!" He thought the baby would approve of that.
The giants ran back into their ice palace and brought out Santa. Santa ran up to the boy and cried out, "Thank you, thank you, my young friend! You've saved Christmas!" A red sleigh drawn by eight reindeer came zooming out of the clouds and skidded to an icy stop. Santa leaped into the sleigh and before anyone could say "Merry Christmas!" he had disappeared into the clouds.
"You can feel mighty proud," said the baby. "You've done a mighty good day's work for one Christmas."
It really had been quite a Christmas, the boy was thinking. He hadn't had such a full day since the day he had stayed home from school with a cold and had saved King Arthur from the treachery of his false son Modred, the Black Knight of the Glen, and the ravaging hordes of the Saracens, Huns, Tartars, and Iroquois Indians, one after another. He looked out the window. It was getting dark already, he'd been playing all afternoon. Hey, he thought, I'm hungry.
Suddenly the marbles were once more marbles; the bottle caps, bottle caps. He put them back in their box. The shaving brush was now not a giant but a shaving brush, and the perfume bottle no more than that. He took them back where he had found them. He rummaged through the shelves and found a box of cornflakes. He poured the cornflakes into the big glass bowl and covered them with sugar and milk.
Hey, this is great, he thought. I'm eating out of the giants' ice palace. Hey, everybody. The giants' ice palace is now open as a restaurant. We are open for business.
He sprinkled more sugar on his cornflakes. "Hey, love does make things sweet," he said. He began to laugh and he kept chuckling to himself all the time he ate. Somehow the food tasted better sugared with love and eaten in the giants' ice palace.
After he had eaten, he went in and threw himself down on the bed. He thought of Thor and the baby Jesus and Jack and Santa and the

giants. Somehow they were all different now than they had been before.

Really, it had been a big day. The Mayor's Christmas Tree Party—he'd almost forgotten it—that had been fun, too. It was exciting down there in the Municipal Auditorium with all those kids pushing and yelling and singing carols.

He thought about the Indians that he had lost. He wondered where they were. That Santa Fe train must be halfway across Kansas by now, he thought. Maybe farther than that, chugging through the winter night. Gee, it might be a blizzard out there. No, he decided, it was a starry night, a clear, starry night.

Under the stars out there in the middle of Kansas, along the top of the chugging train, ten Indians were creeping quietly, five forward toward the locomotive, five back toward the caboose. The Indian chief was whispering, "Men, fellow braves, this is the beginning of the Great Indian Uprising. This train is secretly loaded with Gatling guns and sharpshooting rifles. We are going to capture it."

Suddenly the chief stopped and held up his hand. "Men, fellow braves, I have been wrong. This train is not loaded with Gatling guns, it is loaded with a secret weapon, love. It will take the palefaces by surprise. And all thanks to our young friend back there in Kansas City. We must never forget him. Without him the Great Indian Uprising of Love could never have been."

Then out of the air above the train—or was it over the bed?—eight reindeer and a red sleigh appeared. Santa Claus was leaning over the side, yelling down at him, "Merry Christmas everybody! Thanks to you, good friend, thanks to you!"

And high above everything, the chugging train, the creeping Indians, Santa, the giants, and him, he caught a glimpse of the baby, and the baby was saying, "Thank you, my friend. You've made my birthday a very happy one!"

Yeah, Christmas was the baby's birthday. Sure, and he and the baby and Thor and the giants and Santa Claus and the Mayor's Christmas Tree Party and a trainload of creeping Indians all were chugging along under a starry night in the Great Indian Uprising of Love, and Jack and the giants, and he and the baby, and Thor and Santa, and he and love—and he fell asleep.

Christmas Blessings
from
Unity Books
Unity Village, Missouri 64065

Printed U.S.A.
140-F-7261-10M-11-84